BEAUTIFUL

STRANGER

L. MOONE

CONTENTS

Beautiful Stranger   1
Author's Note   177

CHAPTER ONE

I've been dreading my drive home all day. In fact, that is an understatement. After a long day at work, the last thing I need is to be reminded that I've decided to live in that beautiful, mostly serene part of the world called Ascot, Berkshire. Which of course during this week of the year turns into a hellhole, overrun by obscenely rich people clogging up the roads in their Bentleys, Rollers and whatnot. Actually the Bentleys and Rolls Royces don't bother me so much, it's the hordes of not-so-rich people who think it's classy to hire a Hummer limo that I can really do without.

Such is my aversion that I've even started to avoid newspapers this week, the one week in June that the Royal Ascot races take place. If I wanted to see photos of ridiculous hats and passed out drunk people on the lawn, I could've just bought a ticket and gone myself. But I don't really care about horse racing, or showing off. I would much rather attend a music festival, if I had to brave the Great British Weather in inappropriate clothing anyway.

My neighbors tend to flee around this time of year, but unfortunately I can't afford a holiday. With the way things have been at work, I'd better put every spare penny away for a rainy day. At least tonight will be the last time this year I'll have to deal with this mess, tomorrow is my day off and I don't intend to venture out onto the roads at all until next week when normality has returned.

I'm already looking forward to my quiet long weekend, focusing on nothing but my paintings. All I have to do is get there.

Slowly I make my way through the various traffic control measures set up seemingly to hinder the flow of traffic rather than improve it. I suppose it all makes sense to someone. It takes me an hour to get onto Blacknest Road, which in ordinary circumstances would be about five minutes from home. But these are not ordinary circumstances.

As my car creeps along in its spot within the tedious metal conga line that has formed around me, all I have for company are my radio and my grumpy thoughts. And the occasional sympathetic smile from someone in much the same situation in the opposite lane.

I occupy myself by looking at the flash cars that slowly pass by. Nothing too unusual in this part of the world, various Ferraris, Lambos and of course the already mentioned Bentleys and Rolls Royces of all ages. I almost give up on seeing much variety when something small and dark blue catches my eye parked up on the verge ahead. Twin white racing stripes accentuating its curvaceous body, top down to reveal its cream leather interior. Absolutely beautiful. I wonder if it's a real AC Cobra or just a good replica. And more importantly, what is it doing sitting in the muck next to this busy road?

Traffic creeps ahead and I get closer, there's a man in the driver's seat, arms folded and head resting against them on the steering wheel. He is sporting the accepted race-going uniform; grey waistcoat with a matching hat and coat on the passenger seat beside him.

I don't know what possesses me, but I leave my coveted place in the traffic queue and pull up behind him. Just to see if he's okay—I tell myself—or at least to get a better look at his magnificent car.

Stepping out has me cursing under my breath immediately. Of course I managed to position my exit right in the middle of a patch of sticky mud left behind by this morning's early summer showers.

"Excuse me, are you having car trouble?" I ask. He lifts his head off his forearm which is still resting on the steering wheel. "I was wondering if you need help…"

His pale blue eyes stand out against his face and particularly against his dark hair which is starting to grey around the temples. If I had to guess I'd say he was in his late thirties or early forties, and the salt and pepper look is really working for him. Something seems off, though. I remind myself he's probably just had a few too many glasses of champagne or whatever it is they drink at the races.

"I wanted to leave, but thought I probably shouldn't be driving. So I pulled over." His voice sounds friendly, if a tad uncertain. Everything about him suggests money, from his accent to his clothes. Perhaps the car isn't a replica after all.

"You're probably right, I suppose you shouldn't be driving. Where were you headed?" I ask.

He averts his eyes downwards before answering. "I don't know."

"Right. Where do you live?" I try.

"I can't go there." There's an awkward silence after his response, and he grips the steering wheel with both hands and rests his forehead against his knuckles.

I think for a little while and look around. The traffic jam heading away is still going strong, but traffic moving in my direction has started to thin. If pulling over wasn't already weird enough, what I say next actually stuns the rational part of my brain completely. The impulsive surge inside of me is simply impossible to fight, causing my lips to utter certain words before better sense prevails.

"What do you say, you come with me and we'll figure out where you should be going after reaching my place?"

When he looks back up at me, there is not a hint

of suspicion in his eyes. It doesn't seem to register with him that only a reckless lunatic would invite a drunk stranger home. *What the hell am I thinking?*

"That would be nice. Thanks." He tries to smile but instead his face twists. "Oh God, I feel ill." I hurry around the car and open the car door to pull him out by his arm.

"Believe me, tomorrow you'll really regret it if you throw up in that nice car of yours!" I warn him.

He walks a few steps away from the road and leans against a tree. I can't help but stare. He looks fit, about six feet tall, broad shoulders. Any other observations would be pure speculation though, plus it would be difficult for anyone not to look good in formal wear.

I still can't believe I'm doing this. There's something special about him, tempting even. Something that makes him appear trustworthy and harmless. Still, I'm sort of aware of the possibility that it may all be a clever act on his part and I'm about to let an axe murderer into my house.

Walking towards him now, I can see he has his eyes closed and is just breathing in the fresh air away from all the traffic.

"Never mind, I guess it was a false alarm," he mutters.

"Well then, let's go," I say, "I don't think your car would be safe here, though."

"Mine, on the other hand, nobody would touch if I abandoned it here for weeks. And since you're not fit to drive just now..." I continue.

He doesn't say a word, simply places the car keys into my outstretched hand and opens the passenger door for himself. Looking at the gorgeous car, I decide then that even if I end up hacked into bits and buried in my own garden tonight, it will have all been worth it.

After grabbing my handbag and locking my own vehicle, I sit down next to him. His expression has hardly changed, he shows no sign of concern that he's letting a complete stranger drive his car. I have to conclude he's not all there. I turn the key and the engine purrs to life with a deep, thundering rumble which can only mean one thing: under the shiny, curved bonnet, there lives a huge beast of an engine.

"Why so distracted, did you lose big at the races today?" I ask while checking over my shoulder for a gap in the traffic. It occurs to me that my attempt at small talk is making me sound like a cabbie.

"I don't gamble. But yes, in a way." He sighs.

I'm intrigued but don't want to probe too much. The car behind me flashes its lights, allowing me to merge. After a moment's silence, he takes a few deep breaths.

"My wife..." His voice trembles ever so slightly while he speaks, "and someone I'd considered a friend..."

My question unintentionally cut right to the core of the matter, it sounds as if he lost hope rather than money.

"Wow, I'm sorry. That's terrible." I'm not sure I want further detail but I can't take the question back now.

He shakes his head. "I should've seen it. But I guess I wasn't around enough, working long hours, sometimes Saturdays too..." He turns towards me and when the traffic stops again, I get the chance to study his face. Perfectly symmetrical, high cheekbones and a sharp jaw line. He is gorgeous, perhaps even more so because he looks so lost.

"But it was all for her! I wanted to give her the life she deserved. Why didn't she see that?" Tears are starting to blur those magnificent eyes of his. "Instead, she fucking replaces me."

Well, that's one mystery solved. I guess posh people *do* swear.

"You're right, she should've understood," I say.

The traffic starts moving again and we get just a little bit closer to our destination.

"It was all for nothing." He looks out at the trees and houses passing by, lost in thought again.

Nothing more is said for the rest of the drive; fifteen minutes or so. I pull up into the cul-de-sac on the hill where I live, the three surrounding houses are unoccupied while the neighbors are on holiday. The setting is secluded, idyllic but the actual house is modest by most standards. It makes me wonder what his home would look like, the exact opposite I bet. The gravel makes a crunchy sound underneath the tires as I park the car under the rustic wooden carport which is always smothered in pink clematis blooms at this time of year.

Right at this moment the clouds break apart, letting through the pleasantly warm evening sun. I hand him the keys and we both get out of the car. Rather than head for the door, he distractedly takes a few steps towards the fence that surrounds the driveway.

"Beautiful." He's right, but it's been a while since I really appreciated the view myself.

Perhaps I should try my hand at painting a landscape this weekend.

Tall trees line the fields that cover most of the hill below. The lush green leaves on the trees as well as the long grass glisten in the golden light, giving everything a warm glow.

Meanwhile I open the low gate and enter into the garden that runs along the side of the house. There's a large wooden table and bench set up against the wall, overlooking the same downhill aspect. He follows a few steps behind me.

"Make yourself at home, I'll just go inside and get

some cushions." I turn the key and enter the cozy living room through the patio door.

While I'm inside already, I might as well cobble together a meal of sorts. Rushing to pop some pre-baked bread in the oven, I raid the fridge for cold meat and cheese.

I vaguely wonder why I'm bothering to hide the Aldi packaging, or arrange everything on a nice plate. After all, my bluff is pretty much called already, the classiest bottle of wine I have probably wouldn't have cost more than five pounds. Must've been a gift that's been languishing in my kitchen for much too long.

It annoys me that I even care, I never pretend to be something I'm not, why start now?

CHAPTER TWO

"Excuse me, where's your bathroom?" I hear him call from the back door.

"Oh, please come in, it's just over there..." When he enters, I point out the right door in the hallway.

The contrast between us is even more obvious to me now, he looks like everything I am not in his formal wear which probably cost more than my car is worth. At the same time I—at twenty-four—still dress like I did as a teenager, faded jeans and t-shirts with inappropriate prints. The only 'fancy' clothes I own are worn exclusively to job interviews and then too they're Primark or at a stretch, Next. You could mistake me for a simple idealist, not moved by worldly possessions, when in fact I am just a bit stingy and lazy.

Plus, I've never really understood fashion.

Strangely, he looks quite at home, walking over the terracotta tiles and towards the door I've just shown him. He shoots a few glances at the eclectic mix of paintings and photographs on my walls on his way. Like he's meant to be here, in my house. I try and shake off that thought. He's just some stranger and I'm an idiot for doing this.

The ping of the oven timer brings me back to

reality and I pile all the food, plates and cutlery high onto a tray, and head back out. After I've arranged everything on the garden table and made another trip for the cushions, a water jug and the aforementioned cheap wine, he comes back out as well.

"You didn't need to..." he says with a smile.

Looking at him now, much more at ease than before, I feel like I'm getting a hint of his usual demeanor. Charismatic is probably the best word for it, but still he seems genuine.

"I sort of did, I'm starving," I respond, "and Domino's doesn't deliver here."

He lets out a laugh while sitting down on the bench beside me.

"I wasn't sure what you'd like," I point at the food, wine and water, "unless you want coffee or tea, I can do that too."

"Yeah, I don't tend to drink much, is it that obvious?" He smiles again. My heart is pounding all the way up in my throat. I can't get over how handsome he is, the change in body language has made that even more obvious.

"Well, whatever you need, just ask." My eyes are drawn to his, they seem more turquoise than blue now but that might just be the light. He holds my gaze just a little longer than strictly necessary before picking up the wine and corkscrew.

"I suppose one glass won't hurt. I promise I don't

feel ill anymore." He doesn't look it either, must be the fresh air.

"Don't be so sure, you haven't tried it yet. It's probably nowhere near the quality you're used to," I say, still mesmerized by his eyes.

He grins at me. "Everything is only as good as the company it's enjoyed in."

I feel the corners of my mouth respond immediately, this is a game I can play. "Well, and what do you know about current company other than that I was overly keen to get my hands on your car keys?"

"Firstly, you took a huge risk trying to help out a complete stranger." Winking at me, he adds, "Car keys or no car keys."

I accept the glass of wine he has poured for me.

"Furthermore, I don't recall the last time anyone has made an effort putting together a meal for me..." His gaze wanders out over the field again.

"Fine, if you say so," I say, "but for all you know I could be a psychopath, only pretending to be friendly."

He looks back at me again, the amused glint in his eyes reappearing. "So could I."

"Cheers," I say, raising my glass towards him. "To us, pretending to be friendly."

We both take a sip, stealing little looks at each other in turn.

BEAUTIFUL STRANGER

He's putting on a brilliant performance, like what he said in the car never happened. Perhaps it's his way of dealing with things. Who am I to argue with such a tempting façade?

I offer him the bread basket and platter of cold cuts. He eats eagerly, like he's famished.

"You know, had I known, I would've prepared something a little nicer than this," I joke.

"I'll keep that in mind. To warn you in advance before randomly meeting at the side of the road," he responds.

I eat a few bites myself.

"What's your name?" I ask.

"Peter. Peter Layton."

"Well, it's nice to meet you, Peter. I'm Claudia de Wit."

"The pleasure is all mine. Dutch, eh? I wouldn't have been able to guess," Peter says.

"Well, only by name. I've always lived here." I take a big bite of bread and cheese, realizing that I'm clearly kidding myself.

We eat in silence until the food is nearly finished. Taking small breaks in between bites for a sip of wine and a few covert glances back and forth.

Peter straightens himself and leans back against the bench, arms folded behind his head. It's still so bright, it would be quite impossible to correctly guess the time.

He clears his throat and looks at me. "That was lovely, thank you."

I blush, *how undeserved*. "Oh, stop it."

I look at him from the corner of my eye, wondering if my growing attraction towards him has at least in part to do with the slight wine buzz I've developed. But whatever the cause, the feeling seems mutual, because he's now blatantly staring back at me.

"Claudia." The way he says my name makes me weak inside.

"Yes?" I respond.

"After all this..." He motions over at the empty bottle. "I think it would be even less appropriate for me to drive anywhere."

"You know, you're quite right."

I lean over towards him slightly, seeing him do the same wreaks havoc with my heartbeat. *It's only the wine*, I tell myself. But I'm drawn to him, lips parted slightly, as he is to me.

His face just inches away, I hold my breath and slip my hand over his shoulder, around his neck and keep drowning in the blue depth of his eyes as our lips meet. His eyes close when I press my lips against his. I'm overcome by how soft they are. I want to taste him, feel him closer.

His arms wrap around me, pulling me in. The tip of my tongue finds his lips open just enough. He returns my kiss with a need so infectious it causes my own to surge dramatically. With our tongues entwined, his hands explore the contours of my back. Through my t-shirt at first, but quickly progressing underneath. They're warm and determined, rubbing my tense muscles as if I still need further persuasion. I don't. My own hands are fumbling with the buttons of his shirt, aiming to rid him of it entirely. As soon as I've got it wide open, he pulls back and gives me a devilish look before stripping my t-shirt off me in one swift upward tug.

An appreciative smile appears on his face as he looks down at what he has just uncovered. I'm glad that by some sort of cosmic coincidence I actually wore pretty underwear today and not my everyday rags. My cleavage is practically spilling out of the bright red push-up bra, I know my jeans hide the counterpart frilly thong.

I get up from the bench, eager to move somewhere more comfortable, more intimate. But he has other ideas. As he stands up next to me, his eyes would've been enough to hypnotize me to stay. To emphasize his point further, he slips two fingers into the waistband of my jeans and with a jerk I am pulled tightly against him, his other hand squeezing firmly into my waist.

"Oh no, you don't!" His voice is determined as his hands, I am frozen in place, still looking up at his face.

He starts to unbutton my jeans, I can't wait to feel his hands on my bare skin all over. My fingers meanwhile are running up his lean chest. I have no doubt that he must work out regularly to maintain his physique. He isn't overly buff, but I can clearly feel his abs under my fingers. There isn't a hint of fat on his perfectly V-shaped frame. His perfection begs to be captured in a sketch at the very least, something I'm certain I'll attempt from memory if I have to.

Meanwhile he has peeled my skin tight jeans halfway down my ample hips and is letting his fingers work through my curvaceous ass. I can't match up to his level of physical perfection by quite a stretch, but my soft femininity seems to excite him further. One of his hands has come up to explore what is still hidden beyond my bra.

I continue to study him by touch, down the curvature of his muscular back, leading to his ass. A fine specimen indeed, amazingly firm. As I grab him, hard, he presses forward, encouraging further exploration. I want to devour him, kissing and sucking on his silky smooth skin, running my nose through the little patch of curly dark hair that sits in the centre of his athletic chest. I'm glad he's not one of those guys who gets rid of it all; this to me is the ultimate symbol of masculinity.

His right hand loosens on my ass cheek before travelling upwards, leaving a trail of fire burning along my spine before gently nudging my head upwards from the back of my neck. His breath against my face again, I am overwhelmed by him and his hungry kisses once more. But I don't just want his tongue, I also want what's pressed up against my thigh. His cock as hard and strong as the rest of him through the fabric of his trousers. I'm just about to open his fly and slip my hand inside when abruptly he stops and pushes me down.

He leans with me and slides the dirty dishes and tray swiftly aside before laying me down on the garden table. His right hand pulls my jeans off me completely, leaving them piled up on the ground. His other undoes his trousers and strokes himself, allowing me a glimpse of his perfectly straight, huge manhood which is standing proudly just for me.

I lift my feet up onto the bench either side of him, and slip off my bra straps before opening it and flinging it onto the ground as well. He cannot take his eyes off my hard dark pink nipples which are now aching to be kissed and caressed. So much so I decide to show him exactly how, cupping my breasts in my hands, rolling my nipples between thumb and forefinger. He shows little patience and dives down, taking both nipples into his mouth one after the other, licking them and circling around them with his tongue. It tickles me and heats me to my core.

While one of my hands claws at the smooth skin

on his back, the other travels down my length and into my panties. I can feel pearls of moisture already accumulated on my labia, my fingertips softly spreading it over my silky, hairless skin. I am throbbing, engorged with anticipation and lust, any moment now my perfect stranger will take me in this vulnerable position on the wooden table.

He lifts up to observe what I'm doing to myself, keeping a firm grasp on his impressively proportioned member, groaning with the same desire that is reverberating through my veins.

CHAPTER THREE

"Shit, do you have a condom?" he asks, the cool façade he had so carefully constructed crumbling suddenly.

"No. But I'm clean, are you?" Clearly, this must be the wine talking. I may be on the pill but I only just found out his name a short while ago. If he has any sense, he'll refuse but I am way too far gone to care about the consequences.

"Yes. Are you sure about this?" His voice is trembling with built up tension, aching for release. Even so, I get the impression that he would respect it if I said no.

Lifting my butt off the table slightly, I wiggle off the last bit of frilly red mesh which had been covering the remainder of my modesty.

Giving him my most seductive look, I breathe: "Yes, absolutely!"

The naughty grin from before makes a reappearance on his face. Looks like he's ready to be reckless together.

Both hands locked around my hips, he lifts me and slides me down to the very edge of the table. The rough wood scrapes my back in a sensation that feels appropriately bittersweet.

His huge cock is pressing at my entrance, making me moan in anticipation. He enters me with grace, pressing his hips into my widely spread thighs in a swift motion that takes my breath away.

My insides are set alight and I scream with pleasure every time he enters me, our combined sounds of delight not held back by shame or worry. I feel liberated by his every move; he's playing me like I'm a musical instrument. His hips continue to move energetically, filling me to my core with each deep thrust. The slight upward tilt he adopts as he enters makes his head scrape deliciously against my G-spot, causing it to tingle and burn at the same time.

I run my hands over his torso, feeling his muscles harden in ripples as he moves. He continues to look at me throughout, eyelids half closed but not fully hiding the deep blue sea that lies beneath. I've never been fucked quite how he takes me, his hands kneading my thighs, hips and waist in turn, in between fondling my breasts, none of these unusual by themselves but his touch feels special. Just the right amount of pressure, teasing, heightening my pleasure further and further.

His focus unfaltering, not broken by any worry of being overheard, he is truly in the moment, with an expression so serene he could have been meditating. And his timing is immaculate, fast and sure as he continues to speed up and fuck me as hard as my body needs it. He is so aware of every noise and movement I make, there is no need to speak, he understands me perfectly. I continue to ache for more, panting heavily and raising my hips to meet him in his frenzied rhythm.

"Oh God, yes, I'm so close!" I cry out, feeling the walls of my pussy contract suddenly as I tense up, fingers dug deep into his hips as he pushes deep and hard a few more times, before letting go of my thigh and rubbing his thumb on my clitoris through the shudders and loud screams of my orgasm.

"You're so beautiful," he whispers at me. The tense focus he has shown all along is still obvious while he tenderly caresses my spent body. I know he must still seek release and I'm desperate to give it to him.

I force myself upright and to his surprise push him back and out of me.

"Your turn, baby," I say, while dropping down on my knees in front of him. The cold gritty surface of the brick paving presses hard into my knees, but the pain feels surreal to me.

I grasp his balls and base of his shaft with one hand and lick along the bottom length of his cock. His taste mixed with my own, I softly open my mouth to let him in, testing my limits as I suck him clean. He looks down at me, his eyes widening and closing in turn every time I take him deep into my mouth, now firmly gripping his thighs to steady myself.

It is so obvious now that I'm concentrating purely on his pleasure that he has been holding back for quite a while. A real gentleman all the way, taking care of me before himself. But there is no more reason for that now.

One hand travels around his hip and starts kneading through his ass cheek, the other focusing on his balls which have started to firm up. I increase my tempo slightly, pressing my tongue against his shaft as I take it deep. A gasp escapes his lips, he clearly loves to watch me look up at him with my mouth full.

He is very well hung indeed but with a bit of practice I can get the angle just right to allow him inside me further. I speed up slightly, encouraged by his hand which is running through my hair now. Still the gentleman, he lets me set the pace without pushing. His shallow short breaths act as my guide.

I suck on his head and tease the tip of his cock with my tongue. He shudders and his hips press towards me. I take the cue and continue my deeper, faster rhythm from before, the deep guttural groans he lets out with every movement a sure indicator that I'm on the right track.

Speeding up faster and faster, as I bump the head as far back into my throat as I can, he goes rigid. First his muscles in his ass turn to rock under my hand, then his thighs refuse to flex like they had done before. Finally his hand in my hair clamps into a fist and he is completely still while I suck hard. His balls shrink and his whole length pulsates violently while he gushes into my throat.

I draw back, rubbing my tongue against his shaft and over his head before letting go, swallowing all he had to give. He stumbles back while letting go of my hair and gasps for air, leaning against the backrest of the bench.

"Bloody hell," he pants.

I get up and try my best to brush the dirt off my knees before straightening myself. From behind the long streaks of hair falling into my face I still can't keep my eyes off him. A calm has washed over him, his face relaxing into post-orgasmic bliss. Leaning in and slipping one arm around my waist, he brushes my hair out of my face before another, more tender kiss. When he lets go, he starts to gather my clothes off the ground.

I accept them with a smile, but have no intention of covering up.

"Excuse me for a minute," I say, before turning towards the house. The evening sun is still strong and warms my naked skin, soothing the scrapes on my back left behind by the rough wood of the table. But I'm still riding the high he gave me, knowing it was exactly what I needed so I'll wear these scars with pride.

I turn my head slightly to glance back at him as I open the door, pleased to note that he's still watching me walk up the garden path in a state of full undress.

Inside I make my way to the bathroom, discarding my clothes in the laundry hamper and finding a pair of slippers.

Considering it's not very late yet, I check the fridge before going back out. Fresh strawberries and cream are supposedly an early summer classic; it seems fitting. Through the window I can see that he's sitting down now, arms draped over the backrest and equally unconcerned by his lack of attire. Not that he has any reason to be, as far as the eye can see there's not a soul in sight, just greenery.

Balancing the bowl of strawberries and another filled with cream on my arm and holding onto the neck of another full wine bottle, I struggle through the door and greet his expectant expression with a wide grin.

"Dessert?"

"Why not." He quickly rescues the bottle and puts it on the table while I sit down next to him.

After putting down the strawberries I make a half-hearted attempt to stack up the used dishes from dinner. A buzzing noise starts coming from his waistcoat which is by now hung neatly over the side of the bench. Leaning over, he starts to check the pockets.

"Oh, bollocks," he curses under his breath when he finds his iPhone.

"I'll give you some privacy..." I start to get up but he stops me, shaking his head.

"No," he says, putting the phone face down on the table, "I've nothing to say to her, neither of them actually."

The next minute or so of silence passes in slow motion.

"What are you going to do?" I finally ask, despite realizing it's none of my business.

Luckily my question doesn't appear to offend him. "I don't really know... But I'm not going to forgive her and pretend this never happened."

He leans over and helps himself to strawberries. Feeling a slight chill in the air, I put my feet up on the bench and wrap my arms around them.

"What exactly happened? If you don't mind me asking..." It's not just that I am nosy by nature, but I wish I could get a glimpse of what's going on in Peter's head.

"I saw them, my wife and Chris. After the races finished, the three of us and some more friends went to a nearby pub on the High Street, planning to just stay for a little while before our dinner reservation. By then everyone had had a few, except me because I was driving. On my way back from the men's room I saw them, hands all over each other. So humiliating."

"I can imagine," I respond softly, taking his hand and weaving my fingers in between his.

He turns towards me, the uncertainty in his eyes reminding me of earlier in the car. "Do you really want to hear all this, I mean...?"

"Whatever you want to tell me, yes." My index finger brush against his, hoping to emphasize my point. I do care, even if we've only just met. I just wish I could help somehow.

"Alright, well, God knows how long it's been going on between them. All these years I was clueless and preoccupied, trying to earn enough to maintain the lifestyle she had been craving. Every demand of hers I tried to fulfill. Thinking about it, I can't remember if there was ever a spark between us. When I saw them together it hit me that she wasn't cold like I had come to accept, except around me...

"Had a few drinks at the bar to try and calm down and decided to leave them to it, I was too angry and hurt to face them. I had no idea where I was going to go, and after getting the car I somehow ended up parked alongside that road. And then you magically appeared."

His fingers wrap around mine tightly and he looks at our hands woven together. The tense frown on his face is starting to melt away once more.

"I never strayed once in fifteen years."

"Until today," I whisper.

"Yes, until today." He lifts up my hand and kisses my knuckles.

"No regrets?" I ask.

The same infectious smile he has been using to win me over with has returned. "None."

He takes me into his arms. We kiss tenderly, rekindling earlier desires, but now there is also a new closeness between us. He may have come into my life completely by chance, but I'm really starting to like this mysterious and beautiful stranger.

"Maybe it's not such a bad thing..." I say in between kisses, "getting a second chance, to reconsider what you want out of life. Do you have kids?"

"She never wanted any. You're right, this is a second chance, isn't it?" As soon as he finishes the sentence his smile turns into a naughty grin. Before I know it he scoops me up in his arms. The shock of it all causes me to start giggling uncontrollably.

"Now, where to, my-lady?"

Unable to speak through my giggle fit, I just point at the door which he manages to negotiate relatively easily even with his arms full. Once inside I direct him straight down the hall and to the bedroom, feeling very grateful that there are no stairs in our way.

CHAPTER FOUR

He lays me down on the large wooden bed, the sheets are smooth and cool against my skin. I roll over onto my stomach, with both feet pointing playfully in the air.

"Insatiable, are we?" I wink at him.

"You make that very easy..." He kneels on the bed next to me, his manhood well on its way to grow to its former glory.

Leaning on one elbow, I reach for him, feeling his cock in my hand once more. The touch of my hand against the velvety skin on his shaft causes an immediate reaction, he shifts forward, moaning eagerly. His hands run over my back towards my ass, massaging me. His fingertips trace the fold between butt cheek and thigh. I let out a moan myself, lifting my hips up to guide his fingers where I want them.

He takes his time, caressing my inner thighs right up to my outer labia but no further. After running his hands over my ass cheeks and thighs a few more times, he holds on to my hips and lifts me up on my knees.

"Spread, baby," he instructs me.

I do as he says, spreading my legs apart as far as possible while still kneeling, upper body pressed against the bed and ass up in the air. He positions himself right behind me and grabs my thighs, and the uncertainty of what comes next has me pulsating and dripping with anticipation.

Unexpectedly he plunges his tongue into my slit, deep. It feels so good I cry out into the pillow. His lips close around my labia while he flicks his tongue inside me, making me quiver. I am well on my way to bursting with hardly any effort on his part. He seems not to want to rush it, moving out a little bit, licking my inner labia and planting soft teasing kisses all around. The mattress moves behind me but I'm frozen and unwilling to check what's happening, both my hands are clawing at the sheet beside me.

His hands wrap around my thighs now from the other side, pulling me down on top of his face, kissing the delicate skin around my clit and giving it soft teasing licks with his tongue. Every time he touches me there, I feel like an electric current hits me, causing me to spasm and twitch. But his strong hands hold me in place and within his reach.

"Oh my, you're so good!" I breathe.

He responds by diving into my pussy again, licking me deeper than before. I shudder and gasp for air, feeling the tension inside my lower abdomen build up more and more. Then he stops and lifts me up to get out from underneath me.

"I need to be in you." There's no arguing with his

tone. He firmly grabs hold of my hips again and adjusts my position to his liking.

With the tip of his cock he circles me, teasing me.

"Oh take me!" I cry. The wait is almost too much for me to bear.

He thrusts inside of me and it lights my skin on fire. He finds his same controlled rhythm from earlier, pushing into me with determination and focus not to give up until I'm done. But I crave for him to lose it, just like I have.

"I'm so close," I gasp, "promise you won't hold back this time. I want all you have to give!"

His manhood twitches in response and he lets out a low groan. If he likes for me to talk, I aim to please.

"You're the best I've ever had!" I tense up my arms and shoulders, pushing back into him with every stroke, it's my turn to be focused. "Fuck me harder!"

As I will my pussy to contract around him, keeping him in a stranglehold, his fingers bury deeper into the soft flesh around my hips and he speeds up.

"You're driving me crazy!" His voice sounds choked, still holding back.

"I want you! Out of control!" I scream, squeezing him tighter inside me. It's as if a switch flips inside his mind, because he starts panting heavily, bruising my hips with his fingers that had still tried to be gentle earlier. He slams into me so quickly and forcefully that I can feel the skin on my ass zing after every impact.

I cry out, loudly, so close to orgasm it's killing me. He joins in, still pounding me at a breath-taking speed. Then he tenses with a primal groan, I look around to see his eyes are closed in a gorgeous frown as he's pressed deep into me. It is the most glorious sight I've ever laid eyes on. I squeeze hard, rubbing back against his hot, pulsating cock. He fights his urge to stay still, his forced short thrusts send me over the edge with him. Involuntarily my back curves and head tilts upwards, I let out a loud scream as my body is being shaken by the most intense orgasm I have experienced so far. I feel tears burning in my eyes and my muscles one by one turn into jelly. Peter stops shuddering from his own climax behind me and lets go of my hips. However hard he may have held me, I can feel no pain.

He leans forward on one arm and I feel the other slip around my waist, cradling me. We lie down on our sides just as we are, he doesn't pull out and neither do I want him to.

With his head pressed into my hair and arm wrapped around me, I feel not just satisfied but safe. Lazily I wonder whether this is more than just sex.

Just as I decide I'm better off not overcomplicating things, he interrupts my thoughts.

"Best you've ever had, eh?" The sound of his voice tells me he's smiling, and so am I.

"By a mile," I sigh, tugging at his arm to get it around me even tighter.

"Likewise."

"Don't sneak off while I'm asleep," I mumble, suddenly starting to feel overcome by tiredness.

"You wouldn't get rid of me that easily." He kisses my ear.

"You know, you're simply amazing." I say, while drifting off. His face pressed against my neck and shoulder, right now feels utterly perfect.

***

A quick glance at the alarm clock reveals that it's only eight am. My body clock seems unaware that it's my day off, in any case the pressing need I'm feeling is one I cannot ignore for long.

I get up and sleepily wander to the bathroom, my head still fuzzy from last night's wine excesses but at least I don't have a hangover. *Where is Peter anyway?* The sheets next to me were cold when I awoke but I never noticed him leaving.

The back of the bathroom door hides a satin dressing gown which I decide to put on. One can never be sure whether the postman or someone else will turn up early. When I'm done washing my hands and splashing water in my face, I head to the kitchen. His car is still prominently parked outside and I'm relieved that he's still around just like he said he would be.

I can hear his voice outside now, a quick check through the living room window shows that he's sitting on the same bench overlooking the view, phone to his ear. He is naked from the waist up and bathed in crisp morning sunshine

Observing him for another minute, I note he has a mug and teapot sat in front of him on the table. *Good idea, I could use the caffeine as well.* After a quick trip back into the kitchen, I step outside, mug in hand.

"Morning," he smiles, while putting the phone down next to him.

"Hey," I respond, "you're up early."

"Oh, I guess I'm used to getting up at five every day. Such habits are hard to break." He notices the mug in my hand and reaches out for it. "Tea?"

"Yes, please. How lovely, waking up and then not having to make my own." I sigh and sit down next to him.

"I see you found yourself something to wear," I chuckle, noticing that he is sporting a pair of ultra-girly pink pajama bottoms.

"Well, I was improvising. Didn't want to wake you."

"That's very sweet of you," I grin before lifting the mug up to my lips to take a sip.

We sit quietly for a few minutes before his phone

rings again.

"I'm sorry, that'll be the office," he says, "I'm not there one day and you'd think the world was coming to an end."

"Well, I guess it's good to be needed," I respond.

Gazing out over the garden, I try to occupy my mind with other things rather than focus on the one-sided conversation going on next to me. The call finishes quite quickly.

"What about you, going to work?" he asks after putting the phone back on the table.

"I have today off." I stretch lazily and lean back, conscious of his arm on the backrest behind me. "I don't think I want to go anywhere at all today."

He doesn't flinch, in fact it seems as though he's getting closer to me with every movement. He definitely isn't the one-night-stand type, instead he's dragging this out. I wonder if, no, *I hope* he'll want to stay today as well.

"So what do you like to do, when you have the day off?" He gives me a coy smile.

"That all depends on whether I have company," I respond.

"It would appear that you're in no hurry to get rid of me then." His smile has turned slightly naughty.

"Whatever makes you say that?" I make a very poor attempt at innocently batting my eyelids before grinning back at him. He pulls me close to him and gives me another of his mind-blowingly passionate kisses I remember so clearly from last night. I can't think, breathe, only reciprocate. How has he in such a short time managed to make me so weak? I couldn't resist if I wanted to.

But something else rudely interrupts us.

CHAPTER FIVE

"Claudia? You there?" mom! What is she doing here?!

My eyes open wide in shock and he lets go of me instantly.

"Shit. I had no idea she was coming over," I whisper.

"Umm, Mom? I'm here," I call out, giving him an apologetic smile.

Immediately she saunters through the gate and in our direction. Noting that she's immaculately dressed as always, every time I see her I am more convinced that I received the vast majority of genes from my dad's side of the family, not hers.

"You weren't answering the door, and your car wasn't... Hey, Claudia, whose car is that?"

She's hardly aware of us until she's halfway up the garden path.

"Oh." She gives Peter the visual once-over in a critical fashion which only a mother can get away with. "I see."

He isn't fazed at all and as soon as she's near enough he gets up to shake her hand with a warm smile on his face.

"Mrs. De Wit, it's a pleasure to meet you. I'm Peter."

BEAUTIFUL STRANGER

She is quite flustered, shaking his hand and staring at him too long for comfort.

Meanwhile I'm seventeen again, sat with my head resting in my hands, preparing myself for the inevitable embarrassment which is coming my way.

"Oh call me Liesbeth, please... nice to meet you too, Peter." She recovers herself quickly and gives me a special mother-daughter glance.

"I didn't think that you'd have company, Claudia. Don't let me interrupt anything..."

I helplessly get up to give her a quick hug.

"We were just having a cup of tea, why don't you join us?" Peter asks.

Grateful for the chance for a quick escape, however short-lived, I agree. "Indeed, let me get you a cup."

I go in to grab another mug and some blueberry muffins that happen to be lying on the counter. Meanwhile my Mom has settled in nicely, chatting to Peter who looks equally at ease.

As I open the door I can just about overhear enough of the conversation to make me cringe.

"...about time she found a nice man." *Oh dear God.* Peter winks at me, obviously he thinks all of this is just hilarious.

I put the mug down in front of her and try to change the subject.

"So, Mom, what brings you here today?"

"Oh I thought it's such a beautiful morning, and you have the day off work anyway, I thought I'd see what my little girl was up to." *Ugh, could she lay it on any thicker?*

"Umm, right," I Momble.

"Anyway as I was saying, Claudia..." *Clearly there is no hope of steering her away from this topic,* "I'm happy for you both. Peter, you won't believe some of the guys she's brought home in the past!"

I stop chewing my muffin and try to shut her up with my stare alone, but she's purposefully avoiding eye contact.

Peter, meanwhile, is intent on encouraging her. "Really, I'm intrigued, Liesbeth."

"The last one was probably the worst of the lot, Mark, big scruffy fellow. Too many tattoos."

"Mom!" I yell out.

I can feel the blood rushing into my cheeks and ears. This has to be one of the most awkward situations I've ever found myself in. Possibly even worse than when she gave a teenage boy the 'don't knock up my daughter' lecture before our very first date when I was sixteen.

"Sweetheart, don't worry about it. Peter doesn't mind, do you?" she chirps.

"Not at all." He's still grinning at me.

My flight instinct is well and truly awake now and I can't fight it any longer.

"I need a shower," I say while getting up to rush inside.

"Excuse us, Liesbeth." Peter is up at nearly the same moment, overtaking me to hold the door open.

Once inside I can feel that my cheeks are still burning up. I turn to face him, but can't bring myself to make eye contact, I'm still just mortified.

"Damn, I'm really sorry. I really didn't know she was coming over."

Peter cups my face in his hands, making me look up at him.

"If you'd ever met my mother-in-law, you wouldn't be this concerned." He smiles at me and gives me a quick kiss on my forehead.

"I think I should get dressed and head home. There is so much I need to sort out. You have a lovely day with your Mom." He looks down at me and caresses my cheek while I lose myself in his eyes.

Although I don't want him to leave, I really don't want a re-run of the conversation Mom just initiated outside either so I don't argue.

"Thanks for rescuing me last night." He gives me a quick wink before his tone and expression turns serious. "I don't know where I would've ended up, if you hadn't come along."

I wrap my arms around his gorgeously toned body and press myself against him, drinking in his irresistible scent.

"Will I see you again?" I whisper, before lifting my head off his chest.

"Definitely. I promise," he says and kisses my lips gently. His smile looks sincere, making me wonder if he feels the same magnetism I do. Deeper somehow than just physical attraction.

"Well, in that case, see you later," I say, with a cautious smile. "Take care of yourself."

"Sure. See you soon," he responds, giving my cheek one final stroke with his index finger.

We let go of each other and he gathers up his clothes from the armchair next to us before heading into the bedroom to change.

I go outside again, and pour myself another tea.

"Peter already had plans for today, he's getting ready to leave. So what do you want to do?" I ask Mom.

"What do you say we do a bit of shopping, have a nice lunch somewhere? A proper girls' day out?" she responds.

"Sure, that would be nice." I take a sip of my tea, vaguely overhearing doors opening and closing before Peter's car starts with the same deep rumble I remember from last night.

I'm not sure if I should be sad he's going, but I'm not. I smile to myself, realizing now even more than last night, I trust him. *This isn't goodbye.*

BEAUTIFUL STRANGER

"Mom, mind if we go pick up my car before heading out shopping? It'll only take a few minutes."

CHAPTER SIX : PETER

It's almost over. I check my watch, comparing it to the clock hanging on the wall, as if it will make time pass more quickly on this dreary Friday afternoon. Even a quick glance at the weather outside confirms it's a gloomy October day. It can't even be described as cloudy, just white.

A few months ago, everything changed for me; my expectations, my future plans wiped clean. I like to think it's a change for the better; a fresh start and a chance to follow what I truly want in life rather than just do what I'm supposed to. At five sharp, I'll take my belongings and leave this building and soul-destroying job for good.

Stephanie cheating on me had been the wake-up call I so badly needed. I don't blame her anymore, even though it irks me that she didn't just speak her mind first. In any case, the split was as smooth as could be expected. We agreed to put the house on the market while each of us have made alternate arrangements. It's strange to be on my own again. Some days it's liberating, others not so much.

Checking the time again reveals no progress whatsoever. Stretching my arms and folding them behind my head, I stare at nothing while my thoughts revert back to a more comfortable memory from the same day; Claudia. The crazy, impulsive evening spent together which made me see not the despair, but the opportunity ahead of me. I've been thinking about her a lot, even if I doubt I've had an even remotely similar impact on her.

"Hey, Pete. Thought I'd just come in for a little chat..." Chris closes the door behind him and sits down across the desk.

"Sure, have a seat," I say. It's surprising that his affair with Stephanie hasn't made me hate him more. At first I was obviously furious, but now all that's left is detachment. Plus he's always been a bit of a prick, so really I shouldn't have been surprised."

He leans back and looks around the blank canvas that used to be my office, before folding his hands together and focusing on me. Strange, how nearly a decade of my working life fits into one cardboard box; yet without these little things the place looks barren.

"Well, it's certainly been quite a ride, hasn't it? Seems like only yesterday, when we both started off on the floor and look at us now," he says.

"Yes, indeed." I nod, betraying my real feelings that actually it all feels like a lifetime ago.

"Say, how about you join us for one more little get together; Ascot, Saturday next week for the Champions Day meet? Just wouldn't be the same without you there." It's obviously just polite small talk, not sure if he expects me to accept. But, Ascot? I wonder if...

"Yeah, sure. It'll be good fun," I hear myself say.

"Wonderful, I'll have your name added to the guest list."

I nod absentmindedly while he gets up and leaves my office again. It's a bit short notice and I haven't been in touch with her after that day, the morning I left her place.

Would it be odd, contacting her after almost four months? Pretty young girl like that, surely she wouldn't have been sitting around waiting? While my life has felt on hold—waiting for today—hers will have continued as normal, as if our little encounter didn't even happen.

But it did happen. It still does, vividly, whenever I allow myself a moment to recollect it all. From the first kiss—no, the first flirtatious glance—she reminded me of everything I'd been missing. By the time I had her on her back on that wooden table in her garden, I was consumed by a need to prove to her as well as myself that I wasn't just a suit and a pay check. I could tell that she saw it, felt it.

Her dark blonde hair was fanned out over the rough wood, eyes alternating between shut and wide open. I thrust into her with just one purpose; to give her pleasure. Any sound she made served both as a reward and further encouragement.

The image of her naked body has been forever scorched into my memory. She looked beautiful, sensual and primal all at once. Her skin was flawless as silk, irresistibly soft under my touch. Similarly she had difficulty keeping her hands off me.

At the point of no return, her voice pierced through the surrounding countryside; it must have carried for miles. It makes me smile now, that it seemed to not make a difference to either of us whether anyone would hear.

It's impossible to pick a favorite moment of that night. Once the ice was broken between us, our passion showed no signs of slowing. She fell to her knees in front of me, gazing up almost throughout. She knew exactly how to please, but it was the view that nearly killed me. Her eyes seemed to smolder through her long lashes, her hair cascaded down her back and swept back and forth with every movement. I can't remember the last time I'd had a blow job before that; it must've been years. The way her lips stretched wide around my cock drove me insane with lust.

I'd never done anything as rash, and that after only just finding out her name minutes before. That night was in an entirely different league of spontaneity as I'd shown for as long as I could remember. Although she showed all the signs that she was feeling the heat as intensely as I, still I wondered if I had injected the whole experience with more meaning than it deserved.

Sure, we had an intense physical connection. For me that alone made it special. And she was easy to talk to and seemed genuinely interested in me. Something about her made me want to share my darkest moments from earlier that day.

It's hard to pinpoint when I fell for her, as stupid as that seems. I think it happened before we even kissed; it's what made me want to kiss her. Or was that just lust? I'm going to have to see her again and find out.

I spend the rest of my afternoon trying to look her up online. Earlier I'd refrained from doing so because it seemed inappropriate. But the prospect of coming down to her neck of the woods again next weekend surely justifies it now. With a bit of searching, I locate her house on Google Maps. Her name is unusual enough that she should be relatively easy to track down elsewhere..

Her LinkedIn profile looks empty, as if she only registered because someone told her to. Then I realize I'm an idiot, Chris is on there, with his five hundred plus connections and dozens of rubbish endorsements. If someone asked him, he'd name networking as one of his hobbies. Of course someone like Claudia wouldn't use bloody LinkedIn!

BEAUTIFUL STRANGER

I decide to sign up on Facebook, something I'd resisted for years. Maybe the new me can get to like it. This is what I tell myself anyway, the real reason is simply that maybe that's the sort of thing she uses. *She does.*

Her profile pictures are stunning, every single one of them. Even the one where she's covered in paint splatters; her face, hands, even her clothes. Actually that's the best one. There are a fair few of her in what looks like somewhere in the Far East. I admire her for seemingly living life on her own terms. I let the cursor hover over the 'Add Friend' button. Would she even remember me?

No, this feels wrong. I close the page down again and reopen the map. With the phone already in my hand, I open another window and search for something a lot more appropriate. Firstly I owe her an apology for the long wait; secondly, well, Facebook just isn't my style, yet.

"Helen's Flowers, hello?" says a female voice on the other end of the line.

"Hi yes, do you deliver?" I ask and she answers in the affirmative.

"Well, I'd like you to put together something nice with a card. This is a little unusual but I know the delivery location, just not the exact house number. I hope you can accommodate such a request?" After that I explain the exact location with the help of the map, give her Claudia's name and describe the house to avoid any confusion. I also think of something suitable to have written on the card.

Red roses would've been a bit too loaded with symbolism, so I opt for a mixed arrangement instead. I give—let's call her Helen—free rein on picking out something nice.

When I hang up the phone, I can't help but wonder if I'll hear back from Claudia, or if that ship has long since sailed.

CHAPTER SEVEN

"Mom? Have you seen my keys?" I frantically dig through my purse and look around the bedroom in case I've left them on a shelf somewhere.

"Claudia, sweetheart, how *do* you manage on your own...?" Mom walks in with the keys dangling from her index finger.

"Yeah, yeah, alright. Let's go then," I say.

It's been a busy few weeks and I'm actually really looking forward to having lunch together, just the two of us catching up.

We take her car and head to a charming little gastro-pub nearby. Upon sitting down, I scan the menu and firstly opt for some wine. I could really use a drink after the month I've been having. The place is busy, as it usually is on a Saturday, but we'd booked a table in advance. Of course, Mom insisted on it.

"So, what's been going on with you lately, you look a bit pale," she says, leaning over and brushing a few stray locks of hair out of my face.

"Yeah, just work really. It's been crazy ever since they let a bunch of people go in August," I respond with a bleak smile.

"You're safe though?" she asks.

"I should hope so." *But honestly, I'm not so sure.*

The waiter comes to take our order and soon after places the drinks down in front of us. Lovely.

"Oh, isn't this nice, lunch together after such a long time. I can hardly remember the last time we caught up like this..." Mom leans back in her chair and crosses one leg over the other.

I can remember it all too well. Last time her visit was pretty much unplanned, just like a lot of things were. The memories of that day, or mainly the evening prior have been in the back of my mind for months now. I'd tried not to obsess about it, but they never quite went away. Then yesterday, all of it forced itself back into the forefront.

"What's so funny?" Mom asks.

"Oh, nothing..." I try to deflect by taking a sip of wine.

"Say, you never told me the whole story about that guy, what was his name? Are you still seeing him?"

I have a feeling she's not going to let this topic go.

"No, not really had the time for dating you know," I try, hoping this answer will be sufficient.

"Mhm, not had the time. Claudia, you really are strange. And last time you barely talked about him, as if... He's not your boss, is he?" Mom's frowning, scrutinizing me.

"No, no, nothing like that."

"Good." She takes a sip and then focuses on me again.

"So? You seemed to get along. Granted he was a bit old for you maybe, but so charming. What happened?" she continues.

I shrug, feeling yet another smile form on my lips. *God, this is awkward.*

"I... well actually if you must know, we weren't *dating*."

She stares at me, waiting.

"We, you know... Just hooked up the night before."

A deep sigh and a roll of her eyes later, she leans forward with that expression she gets when I've done something idiotic; lips pressed into a thin line, one eyebrow just slightly raised.

"You hooked up. What, you just took a stranger home from a bar or whatever? Jesus, Claudia, when I saw him at your place I honestly thought you were starting to grow up."

I can't help grinning now, she does have a way of getting out my rebellious side.

"You did say he seemed nice, mature. I thought I'd done pretty well, considering," I tease her.

She shakes her head.

"And after that, you didn't keep in touch? I mean, it seemed like there was something more going on, beyond one night," she says.

I take a deep breath, ready to just burst out giggling.

"Well, he was technically still married. So, no." I eye Mom for her reaction and am not disappointed.

She throws her hands in the air as if to say 'where have I gone wrong with this one'. "Married. Really, Claudia?"

"Well sort of, at the time. Not anymore." I dismiss her implied criticism.

"So you *have* kept in touch?"

"Well, I came home yesterday to find a bunch of flowers on my doorstep and a card..." I smile again. "He invited me to join him at some race on Saturday. Apparently he's divorced now."

Mom sits back, both eyebrows raised and arms folded in front of her.

"I thought I'd never see the day, you watching the races... Are you going to go?" she asks.

I shrug and take a moment to mull it over. It might be weird, I don't know what he's expecting from me. But I *have* been thinking about him, a lot.

"Maybe, I guess. As you say, it seemed like there was something there..."

Our food turns up and her attentions are diverted away from Peter and his invitation. I thought it was rather sweet, clearly an expensive bouquet which dare I say isn't really my style. But it's a nice gesture. And the card... It's actually in my handbag, where I kept it so I wouldn't lose his contact details.

BEAUTIFUL STRANGER

'Dear Claudia,

I know I've left this too long, even so I've been thinking about you a lot these past months. Know that I'm deeply sorry; I'd like to make it up to you on Saturday, office lunch at the racecourse. Will you join me?

Peter'

Underneath were a mobile number and an email address.

I know he didn't write it himself, recognizing the logo on the ribbon as that of a local florist. But reading the note gave me a warm feeling inside. He seemed like a good guy back then. I hope the real deal will match up to my memory of him.

Mom doesn't bring up Peter until we're back in the car after our meal.

"Whatever you decide, be careful, okay. He seemed nice, but a man who would step out on his wife... I'm not sure about this," she says, resting her hand on my arm.

"It wasn't quite so simple, though. Technically it was the wife that did it first. When we met he had just found out and was quite upset by it all..." I mumble, deep in thought and replaying the events of that evening in my mind.

"Oh?"

"Yeah, so in a way, the marriage had already ended before anything ever happened between us," I say.

"I guess that sort of changes things. Still, be on guard, after a thing like that he might be a bit—well, being cheated on changes a person," she says.

I wonder... I guess I'm going to find out soon enough because I've made up my mind to accept his invitation.

Later in the afternoon once I'm on my own again, I find the card in my purse and settle down on the sofa. To call or to email?

It's actually making me nervous. I may have been thinking about him too, but I sort of put the idea that anything would come out of this out of my head. For all I knew he could've reconciled with his wife and forgotten all about what happened between us. His invitation opens up a whole range of possibilities I hadn't dared to consider before.

I decide to respond by email.

'Dear Peter,
'So nice to hear from you! I'd love to join you on Saturday. Just one thing, I've never attended such a thing before, please do let me know if there's a dress code to follow... '

I sign with my name and phone number and sit back. For the first time in four months, I allow myself free rein to relive all those buried memories. Alright, perhaps not the first time, but finally I need not feel silly about it.

Googling his name reveals something which I actually could've guessed; he's successful and loaded. A prestigious position in an investment bank which I'd never heard of, not that that means anything. The address in central London and the fact that it has its own Wikipedia page suggests it's one of those which doesn't make the mainstream news often, but is probably influential in the right circles.

Crap, he wrote office lunch, didn't he...

The situation is starting to make me anxious. Mental note: don't drink too much bubbly and do not get political in front of his colleagues. Or cuss, or generally be myself. Oh God. On the bright side, at least I know my way around a full table setting.

I decide to try and put it out of my mind while waiting for a response, which as it turns out doesn't take long at all. His answer is slightly puzzling, but I decide not to question it. He will pick me up at noon on Saturday and says not to worry about the dress code, he'll 'sort something out'. Well, let's just see what that means.

By Tuesday, I've just about forgotten about most of this. Work is a nightmare, and actually the best part of each day is the drive home in the evening. The snaking, narrow roads are a great place to unwind when they're quiet. It helps that I've always enjoyed driving.

But then I'm interrupted by the phone and my heart skips a few beats. Who would call me at this hour, could it be him? I barely even remember what his voice sounds like. I pull over into the nearest parking space and check, a local number.

"Hello?" I say, "Yes, speaking?"

The posh sounding lady introduces herself as working for a clothing shop on the High Street. Apparently she is meant to deliver some dresses to me this week and would like to know my size.

So that's what he meant. I'm taken aback, but do give her my details and answer some basic questions about what colors and styles I like. She's going to send someone to my house in an hour.

I didn't quite know how to react, so I just went with it. Thinking about it now, it's all a bit uncomfortable. The way she said certain things made me wonder how all this must look. *The gentleman kindly requested that something appropriate be sent to your home.'* Appropriate, right.

When I told her my dress size, she responded with, *'Oh, well. I'll see what I can do.'* As if to suggest that I'm making her job difficult by not being a thin waif. The nerve!

Anyway, I suppose he must not agree with her assessment, otherwise why invite me? He seemed to very much enjoy those curves a few months back.

.

CHAPTER EIGHT

Once home, I tidy up a bit and make myself something quick to eat. No sooner am I done eating, than the doorbell rings. That'll be the dresses. Weird, I've never had someone visit my house to show me clothes before.

"Hi," I say, opening the door.

The girl outside looks a bit flustered, with a large selection of gowns wrapped in plastic in her arms. She just about makes it inside the house without dropping any of them and I decide to help before she has a mishap.

"I'm sorry, we should really have a clothes rail or something for these kind of visits. But it doesn't happen all that often," she says, eyeing me curiously.

I realize I must look quite different to her usual clientele. Though I may live in the local area, my house is fairly modest, as is my wardrobe. I don't fit in with the average Range Rover-driving, fake tan-sporting trophy wives or mistresses who would seem like more likely customers. In fact I hate those people.

This is starting to seem like a worse and worse idea.

She checks me out from head to toe and starts going through some of the dresses, keeping around four or so to one side, and the remainder draped over my sofa. I can't make out yet which one is the 'reject' pile, but I do hope it's the smaller one or this visit may not turn out to be a success.

"You're so lucky, he must be quite a catch. When he phoned the boutique earlier, I thought my boss was about ready to faint. She was practically hyperventilating on the phone," she says.

I'm not sure I still feel lucky, awkward is more like it.

"Yeah, he's great..." I mutter.

Finally she seems to have everything sorted out how she wanted and picks up the first dress and rids it of its protective covering. Deep blue satin, a straight pencil shape which seems roughly knee-length. Not impressed by the weird ruffle on top and asymmetric neckline, but I don't want to be rude so I don't say anything.

She gives me one look and puts it aside in favor of something else. A pink, flowing dress with an empire waist. I nod, *yes, this one could work.* Rummaging through the rest of the stuff, there are more blues, purples and pinks following the rough preferences I'd mentioned on the phone.

Thinking maybe the pink one is going to be the one, I get distracted while she continues to show me more dresses. Instead I wonder how much the damn thing costs; whether it's more or less than my monthly salary. Less, surely—*hopefully*...

But the last option brings me back to reality. Red—not subtly red, but in-your-face red. From the nearly off-the-shoulder, rounded neckline to the form-fitting shape. It's actually quite a sensible design; three-quarter sleeves and only just over the knee. Very classy and yet, *red*.

The girl—totally forgot to ask her name— observes me carefully. She already knows this is the one, it's written on my face. All I can think of is how it exactly matches the underwear I wore last time. I wonder if he'd remember that.

I take the dress from her, feeling the soft fabric against my fingers. It's gorgeous. Trying it on confirms this notion; this is the one. A head turner. She remarks that it's very close to some dress someone or other from the TV wore at Royal Ascot. I barely pay attention to her but am pretty much in love, if that's possible.

Taking care not to get it dirty, I hang it up again and put the plastic back over it. Meanwhile she puts all the others back in the car and comes back with some much needed accessories; shoes, bags, the lot. Since I tend to be rubbish at such things, I let her pick out whatever goes the best. Apparently nude pumps and a matching clutch bag are the way to go.

She advises the classy thing would be to wear pearls with it. I suppose I can just about manage that on my own without spending even more of Peter's money.

It's hard not to stare at all of the stuff she's grouped together.

"Don't worry, he'll be speechless when he sees you!" she tries to reassure me.

Yeah, or he'll be speechless when he gets the bill for it all. Is the color too bold though?

"I feel kind of bad accepting all these gifts," I say.

"From the way the boss lady acted, I don't think it'll make a dent in his bank balance. I wouldn't worry about it." She winks at me.

This does not make me feel any better. But instead of arguing, I thank her for all her help and watch as she finishes packing up her car and leaves.

Should I call him to say thanks? It's kind of late, I decide to just send a quick email. Not that it helps make things feel right.

If anything, past relationships tended to be the other way around; I'd be the one holding down a job, whereas the guys I dated were of the starving artist variety. No wonder Mom has been on my case about what she perceived as entering into a grown up relationship.

Let's not get ahead of ourselves, I don't even know the guy.

BEAUTIFUL STRANGER

***

By Saturday morning, I'm starting to get excited as well as nervous. I have no clue what he expects from this. I don't even know if my memories are right anymore or if I've subconsciously managed to embellish them. Was he really that hot, as well as gentlemanly, charming as well as kind? I suppose I'll find out soon enough.

The long, hot shower doesn't do much to relax me, so I decide to pour all my energy into dressing up. At eleven, I'm pretty much done except for some last finishing touches to hair and make-up. I decide to keep it classy, downplayed. The dress is loud enough on its own.

Then I wait, sitting on the sofa with a freshly brewed cup of tea and a clean towel over my lap to avoid any spillages. Deep breaths, *he's just a guy*. Who happens to be taking me as his date to a fancy lunch with a bunch of other normal people. *Except they're most likely filthy rich and powerful.*

I grab the remote and turn on the TV to pass the time. It doesn't work and my tea finishes too quickly as well.

If I have another, I'll be heading for the bathroom the moment we get there. That's not classy, is it?

Finally it's getting close to time and I slip into the elegant nude colored heels which until now were just sitting underneath the coffee table, taunting me. I really want to feel optimistic, but I can't help wonder how badly I'll stick out.

Sure enough, with ten minutes to spare, I hear gravel crunch outside, making me jump up and head for the window. Damn, I do love that car of his; as much as I hate myself for thinking it, it looks like sex on wheels. Even with the soft top on.

When he steps out, I realize my memory did not play tricks on me. Knowing exactly what hides underneath that smart, slim cut grey suit only heightens my excitement. He closes the car door and adjusts the bright red tie he's worn for the occasion. Coincidence?

I open the door and greet him with a big smile.

"Oh my, look at you!" he says, stepping forward and giving me a hug and a kiss on the cheek. I'm not quite sure how to respond so I just go with it.

"Hello, gorgeous," he whispers in my ear, before letting go too soon.

"You're not so bad yourself. Hi," I say.

I'm still nervous, yet not really. Similar to last time, something about him is slowly putting me at ease. Yet I haven't a clue what to talk about now. The time that's passed has made me retreat; the fact that almost everything about today has put me out of my comfort zone doesn't help.

"You had me worried for a bit, whether or not

you'd be free today and give me this chance," he says.

I could drown in those deep blue eyes of his all over again...

"Why wouldn't I? And what chance?" I mumble.

"I shouldn't have left it this long. But I didn't want to contact you while still being married. It seemed disrespectful," he explains.

Who says chivalry is dead?

"That's understandable, she was still your wife even if things had gone bad between you." He starts to shake his head while I speak.

"You misunderstand. My concern was with you, it would be wrong to leave you hanging while needing to focus on getting my home life sorted out."

He is too smooth and yet, could he be genuine? I hope so; his words have made the hairs on my arm stand up, in a good way.

"And everything's sorted now?" I ask.

His smile says it all.

"Ready?" he asks. I take a quick look around, grab my bag and pull the door shut behind me.

Walking across the gravel in heels without damaging the shoes or myself is harder than expected.

Opening the car door for me, he waits while I sit down and get settled in. It's times like these that I'm glad Mom forced me to learn essential skills like getting in and out of cars in dresses. He shuts the door behind me and walks around to his side.

I take a moment to appreciate the walnut console between the two seats and the dash which is covered in sumptuous cream leather. To think he actually let me drive last time is still beyond me.

CHAPTER NINE

"So it's an office lunch thing?" I ask.

He pulls the door shut and turns the key before answering.

"Yes, we—they've got a regular hospitality contract for all the major events."

"Oh that's nice." *If you like that sort of thing.*

His laugh tells me he caught on to my tone; I really should watch my sarcasm.

"I'm sorry if this is prying too much, but what have you told them about me; who I am, how we met, that sort of thing?" I am starting to get fidgety but I catch myself and instead try to just hold onto the grab handle on the door and look out the window at the trees passing us by. The dense greenery has turned an autumnal mixture of reds and browns. I've unintentionally managed to dress accordingly, how funny.

"Frankly, I haven't told anyone anything. But I suppose that'll soon enough have to change. So, who would you say you are?" He sounds amused and I'm beginning to wonder if he thought this through at all.

"Well, obviously you already know my name and where I live, also, I'm twenty-four and work in a call centre in Egham." This situation is beyond ridiculous and I can't help but poke fun at it. "Other than that, I enjoy long walks on the beach and have occasionally been known to invite handsome strangers home with me."

His laugh is infectious. Could it be that he hasn't thought this through because he's not too concerned about what anyone would say?

"So, what about you? My own research only tells me you're a banker and drive a very nice car..."

"Former banker, actually." He pulls up at the mini-roundabout and indicates right to head into the village. "Other than that, I'm forty-one, also enjoy long walks on the beach and have indeed once found myself being invited home by a pretty lady, but I try not to make a habit of it."

I chuckle, remembering a similar dynamic happening last time.

"Why former?" I finally ask.

"Ah, I guess I failed to mention this earlier, Friday last week was my last day. They invited me today as a formality and I realized it would be the perfect chance to see you again. And here we are." The car creeps through the busy traffic on Ascot High Street, reminding me why I try not to go out on race weekends.

He left his job? Surely had he been let go, they wouldn't have invited him at all.

"Well, I suppose you can fill me in on all the

details later. First though, what if anyone asks how we met?" I say.

He shrugs.

"Might as well stay close to the truth; we met in June, purely by chance, we got on well and after that I invited you to join me today." The traffic starts to move again and we creep into a car park, following the huge grey Jaguar ahead of us. Perhaps it only looks huge from this perspective.

After showing the attendant his badge, we pull into a space and he rushes around to open the door for me. I doubt this will ever get old.

I take his arm and we make our way out and along the crowded High Street. The sky is grey, but it's surprisingly warm for late October. Wonder if we'll be indoors, wherever we're going.

The shops thin out towards the end of the High Street, but the crowds do not. It never fails to hit me how small and quaint the village actually is, right until you get within view of the new racecourse entrance. This is the first time I'm walking right up to it, normally I'd just see from the car, driving past.

The view of the glass and steel structure towering above the entry stiles is breath-taking. I remember the controversy surrounding this new design when they built it, but now that I'm seeing it close up, its grandeur seems appropriate. The crowds of people everywhere merge together into a multi-colored, moving mass which seems to have a collective conscience. Pulsating and shifting forward in the corner of my eye, while I continue to admire the building in front of me.

"You know, I've never been inside?" I say.

"Funny, how it takes a visitor to bring a local to the racecourse," he responds. *Right he is.*

He leads me off to a separate entrance where he steps forward, showing his badge again. After checking the guest list, they let us inside, pointing out where we're meant to be going. Not that they needed to, Peter knows exactly what to do and I just follow.

Past the busy lawn, straight towards the big, shiny construction dominating the view ahead; its most prominent feature from this angle are the banners; 'British Champions Series' and similar. Inside and up a few floors we go, greeted by a few more 'gatekeepers', some of whom recognize Peter and quickly move aside to let us through.

Once we've made it into the inner sanctum of the spacious corporate sponsors' box, I start scanning the room. The demographic is largely male, graying and as yet sober. For a moment I feel reassured that I'm not standing out as much as I thought I would, hardly anyone gives me a second look. The obvious exception consists of around half a dozen women who are grouped together by the window. Checking out the competition is what it feels like, but I'm not certain what we're competing for.

A few steps forward and I hear a familiar, thundering yet cheerful voice, the owner of which soon comes into view. I put my hand on Peter's arm, causing him to pause and turn towards me.

"Oh my God, that's...?" I whisper, keeping my gaze fixated forward at the man with the unmistakable freshly-out-of-bed white-blond hair, who still seems to be very much engaged in loud banter with the two bystanders. In proper old boys' club fashion, all three are wearing identical dark ties with light blue diagonal stripes.

"The Mayor, yes." Peter laughs and asks if I'd like him to introduce me.

I shake my head, *let's not do that*. He places his hand on the small of my back and excuses himself to get me some champagne. I'm frozen in place, trying not to stare but failing miserably when the man with the wild, blond hair steps towards me, introducing himself.

"Oh, hi," I say, for lack of something better to say when he shakes my hand.

"I do hope I can count on your vote in the upcoming campaign?" He sounds just like on the TV. Of course he does.

"I can't, I'm afraid," I say.

This is not what he was expecting to hear in this crowd, his crowd.

"Oh?"

"I don't live in London, so I doubt they'd let me vote..." I mumble.

"Ah yes, right you are," he responds, "Can't have everything, eh?"

He flashes a grin at me, places his hand on my arm and nods once before heading past me. That was surreal. Turning around to observe him continue his cheerful spiel with the next little cluster of people, I wonder how he manages to stay 'on' all the time.

"Here you go." Peter turns up at my right, offering me a champagne flute.

"Thanks," I smile.

He throws a quick glance and nod in the mayor's direction before offering me his arm and leading me out and onto the balcony. Lucky for this time of year, it's pleasant outside and dry. Unlike the rest of the week.

As we start making our way towards the railing overlooking the track, he greets a few more people. I just try my best to look respectable and not stumble over my own feet.

"Pete, you made it!" Another guy steps forward and gives him a pat on his upper arm.

"I said I would," Peter responds. His tone doesn't quite match the other guy's enthusiasm.

He turns towards me and introduces us. Apparently the guy's name is Chris, he puts a lot of emphasis on the word 'colleague'. Oh hang on, *that's* Chris?

The advantage and disadvantage of having just one shared memory is that I've often replayed every moment of it in my head even though I tried not to. I'm pretty sure the guy his wife was banging was called Chris. Shit, I hope she isn't here too; that would be way too awkward!

I hope I do a decent job hiding this realization, covering it with a smile and offering my hand to greet him. He takes it and gives it an old-school kiss. *Icky.*

"It's a pleasure to meet you," he says, to which I give him a nod and respond likewise.

He turns towards Peter again and starts chatting about horses and odds. I tune him out but take a moment to casually get more of an impression of whom I suspect is half of the indirect reason I'm even here today.

Roughly similar in age; in his forties definitely, another dark blue suit, white shirt and another striped school tie, this one blue with a double white stripe. His hair is a little longer, greyer as well as thinner and he's kind of shiny and red-faced. I don't like him; wonder if that's due to intuition or bias...

I decide to leave them to their conversation; if Peter wants to get out, he can excuse himself and join me. The balcony overlooks crowds of spectators a few floors below and of course the track a little way ahead of us. There aren't many people outside so I take a moment to catch my breath and enjoy the view. Earlier it had seemed like the sun tried to break through the cloud cover, but this is looking less and less likely now.

I wonder what time the actual racing will start, and if I can bring myself to care about it. As I take the last sip of champagne, someone actually turns up almost immediately to take the empty glass away.

From the corner of my eye I see two of the same women approach who were looking at me earlier.

"Hello, I don't think we've met before," one of them says, her hand stretched out towards me, "I'm Caroline and this is Alison."

"Oh, indeed. Nice to meet you. Claudia," I respond with a smile.

"Do you work at the company as well?" Alison asks, while now offering me her hand to shake.

I shake my head. "No, just a guest. How about you?"

They explain they're here with their husbands. Something about them makes me uneasy, even if I can't identify anything specific in their words or tone which is putting me off.

The questions keep coming though and I do my best to answer. No, this is my first time at the races and yes, it's all very exciting. They comment on my dress, ask what designer it is and I'm finding myself unable to respond. In the end I explain that it was a gift so I'm not really sure, and excuse myself to go freshen up.

As I walk off, both of them are giving each other knowing looks. The gossip has started.

I find Peter still unable to rid himself of Chris, give him a sympathetic smile and continue on towards the facilities. Funny how he stands out to me. In this crowd of stuffy suits in boring old school ties, he seems to shine.

In the ladies' room, I take a moment to check my makeup and hair. All seems in order. Really, I mainly wanted to get away from the interrogation squad before things got too weird. I hope they'll serve lunch soon. Or at least Peter and I can have some time alone to chat and catch up.

CHAPTER TEN

On my way back after wasting what I assume is a suitable amount of time, I hear some familiar voices talking, mentioning my name. I pause. Sounds like Chris has joined forces with the evil twins.

"Really, I'm not sure this is wise. Don't get drawn in by the first pretty young thing that looks your way, Pete," I hear Chris say. "I mean you've only just finalized the divorce..."

What the...

"Absolutely, I'm sorry to say, but she's just after your money, I can guarantee it," says a shrill female voice. *You should know, bitch!*

I wait and listen to more of the conversation, but my heart has sunk already. My biggest worries about today had focused around what to say if the conversation shifted to something I knew nothing about. Or perhaps if I were to slip up and go all liberal on someone. I hadn't considered this sort of scenario at all.

With arms crossed, I step forward and into view. The two trophy witches exchange glances and slip away towards the bar. What I'm left with is Chris, who has his back turned towards me and Peter, whose expression tells me that he knows the shit has hit the fan.

"Mate, I know it's easy to get carried away. My advice would be, have your fun with her, but then find someone—" Chris gets distracted by Peter's head-shaking and gesture to 'kill the conversation'. "What? You need someone more suitable, so at least you won't have to pay for her wardrobe and God knows what else."

Enough, I don't need this. In one swift move, I turn and nearly knock over a waiter carrying a tray of champagne flutes. With that mishap narrowly averted, I head for the door, head swimming with rage. Who do these people think they are?

In the background I vaguely hear Peter's voice: "Chris, you're such a twat—Claudia, wait!"

But I don't wait, instead I stomp through the door that is opened for me and down the corridor to the stairs. When I've reached the bottom, I just about manage to slip by a large crowd pushing into the building. The exit comes into view and my formerly long strides turn into an awkward jog.

It seems not only the company, but the world as a whole has turned on me, demonstrated by the heavy drops which are starting to fall. What starts as a sporadic and almost hesitant shower, turns more intense by the time I'm through the turnstiles. I stop beside the now-closed ticket office and take off my shoes. I can't walk in these fucking things!

As I start making good progress towards the shops, a car pulls up alongside me.

"Love, can I drop you somewhere?" I throw a quick glance at the guy, a taxi driver, and shake my head.

He gives up pretty quickly when I speed up, with my arms wrapped around myself. I'm too pissed off still to really feel the cold, but the rain is definitely starting to soak through. Also, the pavement is quite rough and small puddles have formed in places, making my feet not just wet but numb as well.

All of the High Street passes me by in a blur, before I know it I've turned off and am just a little bit closer to home. Unfortunately that's where the pavement stops being of much use and a quick look down at my feet reveals that my formerly flawless tights have turned a muddy, soggy brown.

Today sucks. All of this is a complete nightmare. Nothing went how I hoped, and I can't believe I was such a dumb shit that I actually had hopes of some kind. And why the fuck didn't I get into that damn taxi? I'm nowhere near home, filthy and it's still pissing down. And the cold is getting to me. Another car pulls up beside me and slows to a crawl. If it's a taxi, I'm taking it.

"Claudia." *Oh fuck.*

"Just... don't." I try to speed up, not that it'll help. How the hell am I going to outrun a sports car?!

"You're all wet. Get in," Peter says.

I stop, arms crossed, and look at him. This is so fucking humiliating and I don't even know why I'm resisting anymore. I bite my lip, hoping it'll somehow contain all this rage and confusion I feel. It doesn't, of course, and tears start to stream down my face; angry tears.

He leans over and opens the passenger door. "Please."

"But, I've got mud all over me." I sound choked, still holding back because I worry if I don't I might just scream my head off.

"I don't give a fuck. Get in the car." His tone isn't one to mess with.

A quick glance at his face confirms I'd be better off complying, so I open the door wider and carefully get in and perch on the edge of the seat in an effort not to drip all over the immaculate leather.

The moment I shut the door, he speeds up and the soggy brown scenery zips past us as I am forced against the backrest. Retracing the route taken barely an hour earlier, the drive doesn't take long. Neither of us speaks a word. I suspect he's furious, whereas by now I'm just drained and empty. I just want to reach home.

Getting out and closing the door behind me, I rummage around for my keys and head straight for the door. The gravel pokes uncomfortably into my feet. I don't check behind me, frankly I don't care whether he follows me in or not. This whole thing has been an incredibly stupid idea. I don't know him, he doesn't know me. There is literally nothing I can think to say to him.

I place the shoes on the hallway floor and proceed towards the bedroom to grab something dry to wear, when his hand closes around my arm, holding me back.

"Let go," I say. He doesn't.

Rationally, I know I should be concerned now. A stranger, in my house, holding on to my arm in anger. Instead I'm still too pissed off myself, fear doesn't even come into it. So I face him, chin thrust forward and face his tense stare. His jaw is clenched and nostrils slightly flared.

"Claudia, I'm sorry about what they said."

I can feel my lip starting to shake, together with the rest of me.

"You don't fucking get it, do you? Why did you even come back, why invite me there? What did you think, everyone would just get along?"

He continues to stare. I should feel threatened but I don't.

"You just fucking stood there and let that dickhead run his mouth after he fucked your wife behind your back—sorry, ex. You get the point! Jesus, what the hell is wrong with you!"

"I thought... hoped that once they'd said whatever they had to say, they'd give up and let us be."

I shake him off and at last he does let go, allowing me to enter the bedroom and slam the door behind me. After listening for a few seconds, I figure he's not going to come after me. Quickly I take the dress off and put it back on its original hanger. Then I rid myself of the muddy tights and wet underwear, both of which I dump on the floor.

It's definitely cold now and I start to shiver. I grab the first warm thing I can find in the wardrobe and a fresh towel for my hair. Did I just mean what I said to him? Had I overreacted about him not defending me in front of those people? Does he perhaps share their view and I'm just a little entertainment to distract from his failed marriage? And why do I even give a shit? Why did I expect more from someone I hardly know? Someone I actually ended up fucking barely ten minutes after finding out his name. I've brought this all on myself.

I sit down on the foot end of the bed and start to cry properly when I see the pathetic looking wet dress hanging a few feet away. Yep, I feel exactly how that looks.

The door creaks but he doesn't come in. Just stands there, observing me.

"I'm really sorry," he says.

Just let me be, damn. I get up and pick up a box of

tissues from the bedside table, attempting to dry my face with one. It's useless, though, because new tears just keep coming as soon as I wipe the old ones away.

"I never expected things to turn out this way." The anger he showed earlier has vanished and he looks helpless.

No shit. I throw him a nasty glance.

"May I come in?" he asks.

I shrug and he takes a few steps forward. Leaning against the chest of drawers, he squeezes the bridge of his nose with forefinger and thumb.

"Today seemed like the perfect chance to see you again."

Anger flares up in me again, though I still don't know why I even care.

"Why? Please explain what you were trying to achieve with all this. Dress me up in expensive clothes à la *Pretty Woman* and show off to your rich and powerful friends? Because if that was your strategy to impress me, you're more clueless than I thought."

"I..." he stammers.

"Honestly, if you wanted to see me again, you could've just gotten in touch. All this..." I gesture at the dress. "It's just fluff. I don't get it."

"Okay, yes." He raises both hands in a sort of defensive gesture. "I was trying to impress you. Didn't think just turning up out of the blue would do the job. I couldn't be sure what I was up against. The truth is I haven't been able to stop thinking about you and felt I had to give this a damn good go."

That last bit softens me, if only for a moment.

"I guess it didn't come across that way, but it took all my restraint not to punch Chris in the head right then and there. He was bang out of order."

"Damn right," I say.

"The only reason I didn't was because I had hoped to salvage the situation and at least enjoy the rest of the day with you. Also, after today I'll never have to see his face again, which was a calming prospect."

I think for a moment, trying to decide what of everything he's just told me is worth taking seriously.

"You honestly thought you needed to bribe me with gifts and promises of fancy lunches, or I wouldn't be interested?" I blink away some of the tears and look at him, hands in his pockets and staring down at his shoes.

"What do I know? As you so kindly reminded me, my wife of fifteen years seemed to prefer Chris over me."

I see where he's coming from. Despite trying so hard to be self-assured, he's probably been having quite a shit time lately. Wouldn't all of this have been much easier without the games? *Men!*

"Shall we start over? Just us, no smoke and mirrors," I say.

He looks up and the moment he lays eyes on my

hair and face, he lets out a small chuckle.

"All day it was dry, until you walked out without an umbrella. How unlucky was that."

I get up and check my face in the mirror and it makes me laugh as well. It looks as though my eyes have melted and started dribbling down my face. While I start to wipe off the blackness and other assorted makeup from my skin, he offers to make some tea, which I gladly accept.

CHAPTER ELEVEN

As soon as I'm done cleaning myself up, I join him in the kitchen. He's leaning against the counter and staring out the window, taking small sips from his mug. With his jacket off, tie loosened and shirt sleeves rolled up, he is quite a sight to behold. *Was he really just trying to impress me? What an outlandish idea.*

"I'm sorry I overreacted earlier," I say, placing my hand on his arm.

He turns and hands me the other mug.

"No, you were absolutely correct. I'm sorry." When he raises his hand to brush a lock of damp hair out of my face, I am frozen in place.

So captivated am I y his blue eyes, I forget to hold on to the tea properly, before being forced back into reality by the burning sensation in my hand. *Ouch.*

"Shall we sit?" I nod my head in the direction of the living room.

He follows me and we sit beside each other on the soft leather sofa. With my still ice cold legs folded underneath me, I turn to face him and place a woolen throw over my lap.

Mug in hand, carefully, to avoid further burns, I try my best to think of a way to break the ice again.

"I just want to make it clear that I don't care how much money you have." I take a sip of tea and look over, waiting for his reaction.

He smiles subtly before leaning into the backrest and resting his free hand on his thigh. It's frustrating how my eyes are drawn to his hand and as a result linger just a bit too long on the entire surrounding area.

"Well, there goes my entire strategy then," he says.

"How about—and I know this is weird and unnatural—just telling me more about yourself? You quit your job, why?" The mood has largely lifted, and although I really would like to know more about him, I'm also reminded of why I managed so little restraint last time. The wine will have helped, but mainly there's this magnetism I can feel pulling me towards him, it's hard to stay on track.

He sighs and puts his mug down on the table before folding both his hands together. Initially I find it hard to concentrate on what he's telling me, but soon I realize that I actually do care about what he's been up to lately. I really want to hear all of it. Even if he is distractingly handsome.

Starting at the beginning, he tells me about confronting his wife and how easily she agreed to just call it quits. How he then started to think about what I told him: that this would mean a fresh start and a chance to do things he hasn't been able to so far.

BEAUTIFUL STRANGER

Shortly after, he decided that what he wanted most was a career change. Money had never meant all that much to him, it was free time and happiness he was after. Sadly his demanding job meant he had a long notice period to work through.

"So what would you like to do now?" I ask. My question causes an awkward smile and a shrug.

"I was rather hoping to take a little time to figure that out."

Still lost in eye contact, I can't help wonder about the massive risk he's taking. Drawing a line under everything he's known for the better part of his adult life with no real plan, that's drastic. Admirable, though; it's the kind of crazy idea I might come up with if I had the opportunity.

Leaning over to keep my mug on the table as well, I feel his eyes on me. It's a nice sensation, albeit a little strange because I don't feel particularly appealing in my fleecy lounge wear and damp hair. He must be seeing something I can't.

Then he asks about me, how I've been lately, to which I briefly mention the mass redundancies at work and resulting added load on the few that remain. My answer is met with a stare and a pause. *My personal life? Oh, no news there.*

This seems to please him and there is another moment of silence though which he briefly touches his chin before running his hand through his hair.

"I don't want to be presumptuous. Whatever happened last time was obviously mostly the heat of the moment. But I've struggled with this dilemma throughout today... I would very much like to kiss you." The very obvious shyness in him makes me want to squeal, but I don't, instead I just grin.

"Sometimes such dilemmas are easily resolved." I lean forward and indeed any anger I felt towards him earlier has vanished.

He's gorgeous and I want my lips to remember his. Our last meeting was too brief, but perhaps the same need not be the case now.

Pushing himself away from the backrest of the sofa, he comes closer and I'm thrilled. Despite everything, there is something so special about him. It makes me want to forget that we're possibly incompatible in many ways. His hand slips behind my neck and into my hair, the roots of which seem to zing with excitement.

I'm drawn to him, unable and unwilling to resist. His kisses burn into me, warming me to the core. I wrap both arms around his impressively toned shoulders. The cotton of his shirt is so soft, it does nothing to disguise the temptation underneath.

"I'm sorry," I whisper in between kisses.

He responds with more determination as if to tell me I have nothing to be sorry about. Forgetting any semblance of restraint, I crawl closer, straddling him as our lips and tongues continue their little dance. His fingers run down my back and both hands end up firmly on my hips; he seems to enjoy holding me there. He leans into the backrest again, and I join him, leaving just enough room to get at his chest. My memories were spot on, and he hasn't changed.

"Claudia," Peter whispers.

"Mhm?"

"Wait," he says.

I sit back, worried about where his interruption is going.

"Before we do anything else, I just want to clarify my intentions." He runs his hand through his hair and looks at me with a slightly uneasy smile.

"Okay, well what are they exactly?" I ask.

"Despite all the rubbish Chris talked earlier, for me this isn't just about sex. Though don't get me wrong, I've had an impossible time trying not to constantly think about everything..."

I smile at him and wait for him to continue.

"I need you to know I want..." His eyes wander while I adjust my top which had gone all twisted.

"Yes?" I say.

"That too." He grins, still watching my attempts at getting sort of decent.

"But I felt an inexplicable connection with you, it started almost straightaway. Beyond the physical. I need to know if you did, do."

"You realize we might not have much in common?"

"I'm not convinced, and in any case I love that you challenge me. I no longer want to be this boring…"

"Posh guy with the nice car and stuffy friends?" I grin at him.

He laughs.

"Yeah, something like that, though I do quite like that car."

"Fair enough," I say.

"I guess what I'm trying to say is, I really like you. And I'd like to see where this goes."

I put my arms around his neck again, attempting to find the truth in the deep blue of his eyes. He's serious. Though I do have my doubts about whether we're compatible, he seems to want to reinvent himself. I don't think I could resist if I tried, I too felt that instant connection and the four months apart or even a big emotional blowout haven't been able to kill it.

"Well then, let's see where *this* goes…" I lean in and brush my lips past his, teasing him with a soft near-kiss. His reaction is instant.

He grabs hold of my sides, just below my underarms and raises me off him. Within the blink of an eye, I'm on my back on the sofa and he's hovering above me, leaning on his hands placed either side of my head. After a moment spent just looking at me, he gets down on his elbows with his face only inches off my chest.

"You're special, Claudia. Let me show you how special..." He peels my top off slowly, kissing any skin as soon as it's exposed.

I smile at him, a little more reassured about our situation than before and completely ready for a good, hard reconciliation. When he makes me feel the way I do right now, how can I worry about what may or may not happen in future? Here and now, everything feels right.

With one hand in his hair, I try to guide him towards my nipple which so far he is carefully avoiding; kissing and teasing only the surrounding skin. I impatiently start unbuttoning his shirt before lifting myself and quickly taking my own top off completely.

"In a hurry?" He grins, I just give him a look that says it all.

He leans on one arm and takes my wrist with his other hand. Before I know it, he pins first one arm back against the armrest of the sofa, and then the other. I'm helplessly spread and his appreciative gaze tells me he likes it this way.

"I want to touch you..." I beg.

He shakes his head and kisses me firmly, gathering both my hands together before I have the chance to regain my composure. His lips make me weak. I can't take my eyes off his face but quickly get distracted when his free hand finds its way down between us, massaging my thighs from the outside in. Getting ever closer to where I really want to be touched.

I let out a moan and he leans in for a further taste. His tongue slips into my mouth the very moment his hand moves past the waistband of my pants.

"How wet you are," he groans against my lips.

Bucking my hips upwards, I feel a rush of pleasure come over me as his finger enters me. He's good, gentle yet firm. He's also rock solid and straining against my thigh. I try to move around, rubbing my leg against his erection in an attempt to break down his control. It's working because he pauses mid-kiss and his eyes close.

"I want you," I whisper.

He presses his cock against me hard but then retreats. My hands are free again when he leans back and sits on his knees between my legs, opening his belt and fly. I quickly rid myself of any remaining clothes and watch him do the same. We're both naked, except for his red tie. He stares at me, eyes dark and unfocused as he grips his length and strokes himself a few times.

My own hand has travelled down as well, circling my clit and coating it in my own juices. This image appears too much for him and he is on me again, biting and sucking on the soft skin of my neck and guiding his cock inside.

I let out a sharp cry once he's in. He fills me completely and utterly and I think I'm sold on the idea of us. I want to tell him but can't speak through the deep, rhythmic strokes. He is focused on me, like a predator on his prey, or perhaps in this case we're both predators in competition with each other, taking turns to please.

My stomach feels taut on the inside, so much tension, anger transformed into passion. I could cry and laugh at the same time, but most of all I just want to keep moving. I run my fingers down his back and he responds by speeding up.

Once again he takes my wrists and holds them firmly above my head. His movements are determined and mostly regular, except the odd twitch and microscopic pause. He wants to be in control but he's failing. I feel pressure building inside me; waves of pleasure increasing in intensity until I'm ready to be ripped open. Moans and gasps fill the room, which I know are mostly mine.

He continues to fuck me faster, harder. The sofa shudders back and forth and I'm done for. My whole body tenses, and I cry—no, I scream.

"Come with me, I need you!" My fingers cringe but have nothing to hold on to. His hands grip me tighter, not letting me move my arms even a little. I look down and see his beautiful body, muscles contracting and relaxing in quick succession; it's hypnotic and altogether too much. How did I get to be with this man? How come he seems to want plain old me and not someone equally perfect?

He pounds into me, releasing my tension and as soon as I'm clearly done for, he freezes with his eyes closed. I know that frown from last time. I also remember the shuddered breathing, the last twitches. I remember the sweet scent of our combined arousal.

When he lowers himself onto me, finally I have my arms back and straightaway wrap them around him. We're both a bit clammy, but it makes no difference. I let my fingers follow the contours of his back muscles which are starting to relax. He breathes deeply and finds my other hand to wrap his fingers through.

"I feel it as well, you know," I say, "not just lust, but something more..."

"It's strange, isn't it? All of this is totally irrational and yet it seems to make perfect sense." He sighs.

"I know. We're practically still strangers, but I can't fight the urge of wanting to know you so much better. I do like you a lot too."

He raises himself off my chest and gives me a peck on the lips. His eyes linger on my face.

"You should cover up, you've already been rained on today. Being naked and sweaty would almost guarantee that you catch a cold," he says.

"I have a better idea." I sit up and stretch while

watching him get off the sofa, gathering our clothes.

"Oh yeah?" he says.

I take his hand and lead him into the bedroom en-suite. He gets the picture straightaway and leaves the clothes in the hamper next to the shower. I open the door and turn on the water while he just observes.

"Join me?" I ask and he does.

Before long we're once more only inches apart, letting our hands do the talking. Caressing, exploring, washing, rinsing. He insists on washing my hair for me, which is sweet. Our shower is prolonged by lengthy, lazy kisses which somehow feel that much better while surrounded by hot flowing water.

When we get out, he wraps me into a towel and dries me off without even entertaining the idea of taking care of himself until I'm done.

"You know I'm not that fragile," I giggle.

"Still, I wouldn't want you getting sick," he insists, and wipes some droplets off my face.

"Alright, alright. Hey, are you hungry? It just occurred to me that we missed lunch."

"Sure," he responds.

CHAPTER TWELVE

Once again I find myself in the kitchen, trying to improvise an unexpected meal. Peter has meanwhile dried himself and is standing by the counter, watching me, wearing one of my bathrobes with, I'm assuming, nothing underneath.

"So where are you staying now?" I ask, while tossing some cooked chicken and greenery together into a large bowl. *Hope he likes salads...*

"When Stephanie and I separated we put the house on the market and I rented a flat closer to work. But I suppose it's time to move now, there's no more reason for me to be in the City," he explains.

"Are they still, you know…"

"What, Stephanie and Chris? I think so, frankly I don't really care. They deserve each other," he responds. I regret asking but a quick glance in his direction suggests he didn't really mind the question.

"I'd been meaning to ask you actually, this seems like a weird place to stay for someone like you," he says.

"Someone like me can't live in a bungalow in Ascot?" I chuckle, "It's okay, I know what you mean."

"This is the house Dad moved into after my folks

got divorced. When he passed away two years later, he left this place to me and I just couldn't bring myself to sell it."

"Oh, I'm sorry." He places his hand on my shoulder.

"That's cool, shit happens, eh." I turn around, bowl in hand.

"Could you take this inside? I'll come with the rest of the stuff," I say.

As soon as I've collected plates, cutlery and some bread rolls together on a tray, I follow Peter into the small dining area inside the living room. He's standing at the other end of the room, looking at the dresser.

"Did you draw this?" he asks, picking up a sketch I had mindlessly left on a shelf. I turn bright red, caught in the act. I had tried to sketch him after our first encounter. Actually, the one he picked up was one of countless attempts over the past months.

"Err, yeah." I'm not quite sure where to look, such is my embarrassment.

He chuckles and walks over.

"Don't be shy, it's really good." He looks at the sketch again, it's unmistakably him, sitting on the garden bench with his shirt off in much the same position as I'd found him that morning four months ago. I suppose things could be worse, he could've found one of the even more revealing ones. Hopefully I've hidden those better.

We sit down to eat and he keeps stealing glances at the sketch and at me but doesn't say anything else. It's awkward.

"I noticed you have quite a few photographs hung up on the wall, mostly exotic looking ones," he says, in between bites of food which of course he has already complimented. Polite as ever.

"Yeah, I took some time out backpacking after Dad passed..."

"I've never travelled much, beyond the obligatory beach or city breaks twice a year," he says.

"Ah well, that was then. I don't get the chance for much of that anymore."

"We could go somewhere together, if you like?" He looks at me expectantly, making me smile. God knows he does try.

"Sure, that would be great," I respond.

We continue eating our food, talking about this and that but nothing very meaningful. When we're done, we settle down on the couch again which still seems to have that distinctive scent surrounding it, reminding me of our intense acrobatics earlier.

He tells me he's been considering Windsor as a possible new home base and I am quick to support the idea. It's a charming city if you ignore the tourists, and only a short drive away. I decide to help him find potential options online, which takes up the best part of the afternoon.

"Oh my, I need a break." Peter stretches himself and leans back into the sofa.

Meanwhile I'm in a similar state, rubbing my eyes while closing the lid of the laptop.

"We've made good progress, though," I say. "With a bit of luck one of these could be your new home."

He takes my hand and pulls me close. The warmth of his arm around me has an immediate effect.

In between subtle but increasingly naughty kisses we decide he should stay the night today, and tomorrow. On Monday while I'm at work he can continue the house hunt from here rather than driving back and forth from central London.

"But no more work today, I've got a much better idea." I turn towards him, grabbing hold of the collar of the fleecy robe he's wearing.

After a hurried kiss, I get up and gently tug at his hand to follow. The bedroom will be the perfect place for an evening of lazy lovemaking and even lazier pillow talk.

Let's just see where this thing between us will go; I've decided to keep an open mind. And indeed I really do like him, a lot. Every time I look into his eyes, the feeling increases. With every kiss, it seems I am drifting away further and further out to sea and away from steady ground. But for some reason that doesn't scare me.

We started off without care for the consequences,

as strangers by the side of the road. Now isn't the time to back down. I expect after Monday, the wait to see Peter again will be a lot shorter than four months, and I'm really looking forward to it.

CHAPTER THIRTEEN

I grip the steering so tightly my knuckles show white. *Of all times, don't you do this to me now!* Sadly the car doesn't listen to me, there is still this terrible screeching sound coming from the engine when I turn the key, but nothing further. It won't bloody start.

After the shit day I've had, with yet further positions hanging in the balance at work, the last thing I need is a big repair bill. I check my watch, quarter past six. Damn, at this rate, I'll be late as well.

Peter has been doing his best to vacate his London flat, selling off most of his stuff and storing the rest of it in my garage. A *life makeover*, he calls it. He wants to rid himself of reminders of his old life, in order to make room for the new. Tonight he's finally coming back with the last load of books or whatnot, ready to move everything into the first suitable place he's able to find in Windsor.

And now I won't even be at home to receive him when he gets there. Goddammit.

Just looking at the to-let ads with him last weekend had made me uneasy. If I didn't have Dad's old house here, I'd never be able to afford to live anywhere one third as nice as what he's considering. Of course I didn't say anything, he can decide for himself how much he's willing to spend. But some of the rents did make me wonder how long he could afford to live around here while he figures out what it is he wants to do next. Surely his resources can't be endless.

I dig around in my handbag, looking for my phone. Of course my breakdown coverage has expired, so I can't even call anyone to fix this issue right now. I'll have to leave the car here over the weekend and find another way home.

Just call a cab, Peter would say. I know he would. *Call a cab, don't worry about the cost, I'll cover it.*

Looking around the parking, I barely recognize any of the cars still left here. Most of the people I get along with have already gone home. It's only then that I see Diane, our team leader, exit the front doors of the office building. I decide to make a run for it, trying to catch her before she escapes too.

"Hey, wait up!" I shout, while trying to collect my bag, the car keys, as well as my coat, trying not to let the wind close the car door in my face.

Diane looks around for a moment as if trying to place the sound of my voice, then pauses when she notices me hurrying towards her.

"Thanks. Hey, my car won't start. Would you mind giving me a lift?" I ask, out of breath, after almost dropping half my stuff on the way from the car.

"Sure thing, but I do need to head into town for a bit first, buy some groceries." Diane checks her watch, then watches me as I try to put on my coat, my hands already shaking in the sharp November wind.

"Okay, thanks a million. I need a few things myself."

As we head into Egham town centre on foot, I send a quick message to Peter, letting him know where I am and where I've hidden the spare key. He doesn't respond, suggesting he's driving. I hope he won't end up waiting for me for too long.

***

When I walk up the gravel drive past Peter's car, my worries of how very late I am are interrupted by the abrupt opening of my own front door.

"Claudia!" Peter greets me with an enthusiastic hug, and takes the bag of groceries from me, allowing me to kick off my muddy shoes before stepping all the way inside. I don't even know why I was nervous at all, considering how pleased he looks to see me.

"Hey you!" I smile at him, thrilled to bits even though we've only spent a few days apart. Somehow every moment away from one another feels like an eternity. I take a moment to just check him out top to bottom, how different he looks in jeans compared to formal clothes.

"So, what happened?" He puts the groceries down on the side table and helps me out of my warm coat, while I start telling him about my ordeal with the car.

"It's never done this before, I don't understand," I complain.

He just looks at me for a moment, as if he knows something I don't.

"These things happen. It's an old car."

I'm about to protest when I realize that in normal people's terms, yes, fifteen years is pretty old for a beat up little hatchback. But I've always had it, and as such am mostly blind to these things.

"It just needs a little TLC. That's all."

I take off my scarf and woolly hat and enjoy the feel of the warm indoor air against my cold skin. I have always had a love-hate relationship with winter. On the one hand there's nothing prettier than a frosty sunrise, when even the tiniest blade of grass seems to shimmer in the sunlight. But it's just too damn cold for my liking, and it tends to take me ages to warm up after a day in a badly designed, insufficiently heated office.

Peter watches me as I rub my hands together and blow some warm air into them.

"Shall I light a fire?" he asks. My smile says it all.

I follow him into the living room, and try my utmost to shed the remaining tension that's deposited itself right in the pit of my stomach, after today's announcements at work. More redundancies are coming, they are going to downsize considerably within the next months.

"What's wrong?" Peter asks, as soon as he's finished with the fireplace and notices my tense expression.

"Just work stuff," I try to brush away his question.

"That doesn't sound good."

All I want is for all that stuff to go away, for the two of us to have a nice evening together, even if all I've brought as nourishment is frozen pizza. The last thing I need is to talk about work crap, so I just shrug. Luckily he backs off the work questions and just takes my hand.

"So it's all done. I've given the keys back this afternoon." Peter runs his fingers over my knuckles, making my heart surge with excitement. "Looks like we'll be seeing a lot more of each other now."

The prospect makes me smile. We've agreed that it's too early to move in together, but while he continues to look for a new place, I'm more than happy for him to stick around.

"Have you found anything promising yet?" I ask.

He nods. "A few flats, yes. The agency is sending someone this weekend for viewings. Perhaps you'd like to come along?" His intense stare burns into me, and I know he's only half thinking about flats and lettings agents. Most of his attention is firmly on me and I love it.

"Since I got back so late, all I've got for dinner is pizza… I hope you don't mind."

"Not at all." Peter takes a step forward and wraps his arms around me until I gladly surrender. "I know just the thing to build up an appetite."

"Oh yeah?" I grin just when he tries to plant a kiss on my lips, which again makes him smile.

"Sexercise. Perhaps you've heard of it?"

I let out a chuckle and pull him tighter against me.

"Sounds familiar, why don't you show me how it works?"

Before I get the chance to do anything further, he scoops me up into his arms and deposits me right on top of the sofa facing the open fire. He makes it seem effortless, even though I'm not that light. We don't get the chance to sample the frozen supermarket pizza until much later in the evening, but neither of us mind the delay.

***

"Say, would you feel weird if I had a bunch of friends over Sunday night?" I ask, while checking the various messages on my phone. Some of my school friends are going to be in the neighborhood shortly, and it would be unfortunate to miss the chance for a reunion. It would also be a great chance for me to reminisce and relive some of the good old days when life seemed a lot simpler.

"Not at all," Peter says, while finishing up an email on the laptop. "There, all done. Once they check my references, I should be getting the keys shortly."

The past week has been all about compromise and adjustment. Although the situation with Peter is only temporary, we've made great progress towards establishing a harmonious living environment. Sure, he's just a house guest, but it's impossible to keep things so casual when you're in a relationship together. The closet in my bedroom has changed from a dumping ground for all my crap, to being almost equally shared between the two of us. There are two toothbrushes in the glass by the sink, and we've even picked sides in bed.

We've also been sharing the chores, which has been quite a relief for me because I hate cleaning at the best of times. Despite all that, it's still weird having him drive me to and from work, now that my car is still in the shop. He hasn't complained even once, but sometimes the way he looks at me when I give him updates about the car repairs suggests there's something he's dying to say but holding back on.

"Great, I'll let them know. I think you'll get along very well." Although I am mostly trying to convince myself rather than him, I'm not all that certain that my crazy friends will mingle well with Peter. The problem certainly won't be at his end, he's always charming in company. No, it's my friends I worry about, they all have very distinct ideas about life and love.

He looks up and winks at me.

"These friends, any chance I'll recognize some of them?" He motions over at some of the pictures scattered around the living room.

"Actually, yes," I say, before getting up and grabbing one group shot from the mantel. "This one has everyone." I point out the various people in the shot to him; Caroline, Jean, Alice... "It was taken in Vietnam." Running my finger over the frame, I can't suppress a smile. We did have a good old time backpacking, the four of us.

Peter leans over and inspects the picture, then puts his arm around me.

"Maybe one day we'll have our own photos to add to your collection."

Yes, maybe, hopefully. Though the car is well on its way towards wiping out what little savings I had, making an exotic holiday seem completely beyond reach.

"I have an idea, how about once I get settled in my new place, we plan a little road trip? Find a nice little country inn somewhere, Kent maybe..." Peter pauses and looks over at me. "Only if you want, of course."

I realize my face must be betraying the conflict

going on inside my head. Kent sounds nice, but I'm well on my way towards being desperately broke. I hate it when my savings fall below a certain level so simply the idea of going on a trip is making me panic.

"Sounds great, but I'm not sure I can afford a trip just now…" I explain. Hopefully he doesn't think I'm dissing his idea, it's just that the timing isn't brilliant.

"My treat. Don't worry about a thing."

I smile bitterly at him. He means well, but I'm not sure I want to accept the offer. Best to let the topic lie until later, so I just nod quickly and put the Vietnam photograph back where it belongs.

The rest of the evening is spent for the most part with both of us working on our own separate plans. He's looking at van rentals to move his things into the new place, while I'm planning what to serve for Sunday's get-together. It's already eleven by the time we end up in bed. Although we're too tired to make love, we never do miss the chance to fall asleep in each other's arms.

CHAPTER FOURTEEN

As foreseen, Peter's references check out and come Saturday afternoon, his phone rings. Overhearing only half the conversation suggests it's the lettings agent about collecting the keys. Peter is visibly excited while setting the meeting, but I'm suddenly overcome with a bit of melancholy.

"Would you like to come along?" he asks, after hanging up the phone.

"Sure." I smile, even though I can't shake the sadness at the prospect of him moving out again. It has been nice having someone around, especially someone as surprisingly easy going as Peter. It's been a while since I've been in a proper relationship, and although everything moved way too quickly, I felt like this thing between the two of us could actually work out.

"I promise you'll love it, you can even see the castle from one of the windows."

Ah yes, castle view. That will have pushed the rent up considerably.

"What time are you getting the keys?" I ask.

"Whenever I get there."

There's a moment of silence as I think of

something appropriate to say.

"I guess it's time to start thinking about a house warming gift then," I remark.

Peter steps forward and takes me into his arms. "Don't you have a whole shed full of potential house warming gifts already?"

He has a point. I've been painting and sketching for the better part of my life, and have collected quite a few finished pieces.

"I didn't realize you've been in the shed," I say.

He smiles mysteriously. "I had to do something to amuse myself while you were at work. And anyway, it's a shame to leave them in there unseen and unappreciated."

"You think so? I mean you would want a painting, of all things?" For a short while growing up, I had entertained the idea of following in Dad's footsteps, becoming an artist just like him, but the charm of that quickly wore off when I saw how his choices affected Mom, and caused them to drift apart. Plus, I never believed that people would actually pay to see my work.

Peter cups my face and plants a kiss on my lips.

"Why not? You're extremely talented."

I know he's just saying that because he likes me, but his compliments make me smile anyway.

"In that case, you can have any canvas you like."

He shakes his head while still staring deeply into

my soul.

"You pick. That way it'll mean more," he says.

I can't wipe the smile off my face. He sure knows what to say, the smooth talker, but he does have a point. I'll see his place this afternoon, and then I'll choose a painting to give him. He'll be the first person, other than family, to hang an original *Claudia de Wit* in his house. The prospect is both exciting as well as a little nerve-wracking. I hope he likes what I'll come up with.

"Sure." I force a smile. "Let's go whenever you're ready."

He nods and puts on a coat, smiling widely at me. "Ready when you are."

I follow suit and before we know it, we're zipping along familiar roads until we reach the edge of Windsor, where traffic starts to slow us down.

"It's been a while since I've last been to Windsor," I remark.

Peter lets out a short laugh. "Don't tell me that in all the time you've lived in the area, you haven't been to the castle, though? Like how you hadn't been inside the race course before I invited you."

"Don't be ridiculous," I say with a grin. "Everyone has been to the bloody castle." *Even if it was just for a school trip.*

"Okay then." A quick look in his direction reveals that he's still grinning.

BEAUTIFUL STRANGER

The traffic ahead starts to clear up and he pulls away, navigating through the various narrow streets like a local. He must have gotten quite familiar with the route, viewing the various flats that caught his eye online. We zigzag through the older part of town for another five minutes, before coming to a halt.

"Here we are." Peter parks neatly inside a bay marked 'residents only'. The lettings agent—clad in the obligatory blue suit, ridiculous tie and brown leather shoes—is already waiting by the main door of the apartment complex.

"Here you go, Mr. Layton," he says, while handing Peter a bunch of keys and a completed rental contract.

"Just a couple of signatures needed and I'll let you get settled in."

I keep looking around, taking mental note of the various luxury cars parked around the area, as well as the squeaky-clean, glass-clad façade of what is going to be Peter's new home. Looks posh, expensive. Best not ask how expensive.

Once the paperwork is done, the lettings agent says his goodbyes and leaves us alone.

"You first," Peter says, unlocking the main door and holding it open for me.

I step inside and am again overwhelmed by how clean and shiny everything is. It looks nothing like other apartment buildings I've been inside, visiting friends.

"Fourth floor." He presses the button and the lift doors open, guiding me inside to select the correct floor.

Once we reach it he uses another key to unlock the front door, and a vast living area opens up ahead of us. The wooden floor looks like it might actually be real, not laminate, and indeed there is a wonderful view through the large French windows leading to the small balcony outside. Perhaps it only looks huge because there's no furniture yet, I try to convince myself, but I already know I'm deceiving myself. It's massive.

Peter's new place is the exact opposite to my house, which looks dark and pokey in comparison. But I like it that way, this open bright space makes me feel exposed and vulnerable.

"Nice, so airy," I remark, while moving through the living room and into the spacious kitchen, with its granite worktop and white glossy cabinets.

"Glad you like it." Peter puts his hand on my shoulder and gently gives it a squeeze, making me feel all warm and fuzzy inside. I guess I could get to like it, in time. Then again, I'm not going to live here so it doesn't really matter what I think.

Though it's not quite what I'm used to, looking around some more at the views, including the one of the castle from the bedroom window, does inspire me. I can't wait to get home and start working on a little something to brighten up these blank, white walls. An already existing painting just won't do.

"If you wait here for a minute, I'll be right back," I say, without giving Peter much of a chance to react, leaving him with a puzzled expression on his face.

I rush out the door, down the elevator and all the way out and quickly make my way towards the small supermarket I'd noticed opposite the parking lot. Though I haven't moved in a while, my friends and I have always had a little tradition, one I'm keen to carry on with Peter now. I make the necessary purchases and rush back to his new flat, where he's already waiting in the doorway.

"Here. Now we can celebrate," I say, while handing him the small chocolate cake and paper napkins I'd bought.

"Excellent." He accepts my rather simple offering with a wide grin, and starts opening up the box, while I take off my coat, spreading it on the floor so that we have somewhere to sit.

"Hope this place turns out to be everything you want it to be. To your new life." I hold up a chunk of cake, as though making a toast, and he does the same.

"It already is all I want it to be," Peter says, eating his bite and leaning over to give me a kiss on my lips as soon as I've finished mine. I wrap my arms around him with a giggle, and within a split second I'm on my back, and he's on top of me, kissing me deeply. Our hands are sticky, leaving little smudges of chocolate on each other's faces, but none of that bothers us. All we can focus on is our lips connecting, tongues as well as limbs entwined until we've found our release. The only time we pause our lovemaking is to feed each other further little mouthfuls of chocolate, the richness and sweetness adding to our pleasure.

Yes, visiting Peter's new flat for the first time definitely does inspire me on multiple levels.

***

Later Saturday evening, I'm back at home, and on my own for the first time in a couple of weeks. Peter is sorting out a few things, taking the obligatory trip to one of the big do-it-yourself stores in the area, and I decide to make a start on his housewarming gift.

His place was light, the view was vast, endless, a lot of sky, a lot of space. Sitting on the paint-stained stool in the middle of my modest shed, I close my eyes and let the mental images flow. I can see waves, clouds, mysterious distant lands. Blues, purples, greens fill my mind, until I'm ready to begin.

I pick up the palette and start with broad strokes until the beginnings of shapes cover the formerly empty canvas. With every passing movement of my brush, the image builds up further, until hours later,

BEAUTIFUL STRANGER

I'm exhausted, yet fulfilled. It's been a while since I've done any painting, and I hadn't realized how much I missed it.

Creating, seeing something appear where there was nothing before, that's always been my outlet. When you get busy with life, spend most of your time with another person, it's easy to forget about what makes us tick deep inside.

The months we'd spent apart, after the first time Peter and I met, I'd whiled away many hours in here, sketching his face, his body, along with random shapes and colors that reminded me of how I'd felt when I was with him. Now that I actually had him, it seemed a lot less necessary to hide myself away in here.

But it was necessary. Painting is a part of me, always will be.

I squint and look at the painting. It's unmistakably the sea, with the suggestion of islands in the background. There are also shapes in the waves, as well as the clouds, that remind me of bodies, engaged in a passionate dance.

Someone with a different outlook could easily see something else in it, that's the whole point. Art isn't objective, its meaning changes from person to person. That's the funny thing, I could paint something with one meaning in mind, but it takes on a life of its own after it's laid down on paper or canvas.

I wipe my hands somewhat clean, although most of the stains on my hands are going to remain for at least a week, and head back into the house.

Things may have started off weird, but today has been a great success. Perhaps with Peter moving into his new place, we can find a balance between our new relationship and us as individuals.

He needs to figure out what he's going to do with his life now, and I'm going to need my alone time to paint.

CHAPTER FIFTEEN

Sunday passes in a blur. After presenting Peter with his gift over breakfast, and a quick trip to the shops for the necessary supplies, party preparations take up most of my afternoon.

It's just after six when the doorbell rings and I can see Caroline and Alice walk up past the kitchen window, straight towards the door. Shortly after, Jean follows from the rear of the car.

Shit, they're here!

"Shall I get it?" Peter asks.

I turn around, my hands still covered in meat marinade and give him a grateful nod. "If you could."

Taking a deep breath, I continue to transfer the chicken kebabs one by one from their plastic tray into the grill. Oh well, I may not be the best hostess, as demonstrated by the fact that I'm still messing about with food when my guests are at the door, but at least I've got help.

"Come in, Claudia is just in the kitchen." Peter greets everyone, their voices slightly more muffled than his.

They must be surprised to see him—or anyone other than me—answering the door upon their arrival.

Just when I'm washing my hands, all three of my friends wander into the hallway leading to the kitchen, giving me all sorts of looks when they notice me.

"Hey! How are you guys? Been a long time," I say, while doing my best to give everyone hugs without dripping water from my freshly washed hands on their backs.

"Not bad. Looks like we have some catching up to do, eh?" Alice remarks, while stealing glances in Peter's direction.

"How about something to drink?" he asks, causing everyone to once again turn and look at him. All three of them are having trouble disguising how taken aback they are. I suppose I could've taken the time to mention this recent change in my love life to them, but in the short back-and-forth setting up tonight's get-together, it just didn't come up. Plus, what was I supposed to do, send a memo? *No longer single, party will include one male guest.* That's ridiculous.

"A drink would be great, wouldn't it, Caroline?" Jean answers, while prodding her in the side with her elbow.

"Uhh, yeah. Thanks…" Caroline straightens herself and tries to stop staring.

"Peter. That's Peter. And this is Caroline, Alice and Jean," I quickly remember to introduce them.

"Nice to meet you," Alice says, holding out her hand much more coyly than generally fits her outgoing character.

"Where did Claudia find you, and do you have any single brothers?" Jean says with a wink, causing giggle fits in the other two girls. *Good Lord, here we go.*

One look in Peter's direction makes me forget my embarrassment. Of course, he's being a very good sport about it all.

"Well, it all began on a rather moist evening back in June," Peter begins, while he starts pouring wine for everyone. He tells the story in broad strokes almost as it happened, but without making it sound as stupid and irresponsible as it really was.

"Cheers," everyone erupts, as soon as the filled glasses have made it around the room. "To Claudia, finally having a social life," someone remarks.

"To all of you people for finally showing your faces around here," I butt in.

Peter remains quiet, with a hint of a smile on his face as he takes the first sip. I can't remember the last time I introduced a boyfriend to this lot. All things considered, it's going pretty well.

"Okay, so who's hungry?" I ask, and am immediately met with applause. Everyone, apparently.

The chicken kebabs will take another five minutes, but I invite them all into the kitchen to help themselves to the bread rolls, salads and various cold snacks. Once everyone has taken what they want, I serve the chicken and we head into the living room together. Conversation flows easily from then on, however Jean does spend an inordinate amount of time interrogating Peter about all sorts, mainly his job, which at the moment is non-existent.

Meanwhile, I chat to Alice about how her writing is going. Apparently she's built up quite the blog following since the last time we've met.

The more the wine flows, the more our chatter comes back to stories of our travels when we decided to take a gap year together, before figuring out what we were going to do with our lives. Every so often, I sit back and just listen in to everyone talking, telling little anecdotes, only half of which I can actually remember, and realize how lucky I was to have such awesome friends. I certainly wouldn't have gone backpacking on my own, I was so nervous about everything back then.

As I lean back in my chair, enjoying the last couple of sips of my third glass, my eyes are drawn to Peter, who is quietly listening in to our conversations. There's a certain wistfulness in his eyes, he seems to be drinking in the story of the hotel owner in Hanoi, trying to put us up in his overpriced cockroach-infested hovel of a room, assuming we wouldn't know any better. Or the time we thought the bus conductor had run off with our luggage…

Although panic-inducing at the time, all these things did make for funny stories now, years later.

BEAUTIFUL STRANGER

"We should do it again," Alice says, while fidgeting with a few peanuts left in the small bowl on the table in between us.

"Yeah. Definitely," I say, while still observing Peter. He's staring right at me now, I know what he's thinking. He wants the same thing. The two of us, exploring the world together. *Maybe one day.*

As soon as everyone is done eating, we leave the dining area in favor of the more comfortable living room. Squeezed together on the couches, we share newer stories, of work, horrible bosses, worse boyfriends and difficult parents. I can't help myself and tell everyone about when Peter and I had just met and Mom turned up out of the blue. Funny how what was once super-embarrassing and awkward has become hilarious in retrospect. Peter jumps in with Mom's remark about the type of guys I would bring home, much to everyone's enjoyment.

We sit around the now lit fireplace—thanks to Peter—for hours, until night threatens to turn to morning. Shortly after three we decide to call it a night, after all, everyone has work in the morning and Alice especially has quite a drive ahead of her to get home.

"Thanks for coming by, I had a lovely time," I say while giving all three of them hugs.

"Same here," Caroline says before heading out to Alice's car.

"You know, he's not bad," Alice whispers in my ear as she's about to go outside too. "At first I thought oh God, Claudia's gone and got herself a sugar daddy. But he's okay."

Glancing quickly in Peter's direction, who is helping Jean into her coat and oblivious to our little moment of gossip, I can't help smiling.

"Yeah, he's a good guy."

"I'm happy for you anyway." Alice gives me a couple of pats on my back before stepping out, and Jean follows behind her.

"Let's do this again sometime." I wave them goodbye, and lean into Peter, who puts his arm around my shoulder.

"Bye!" All three of them wave back at me and soon after, the car pulls out of the drive.

I turn towards Peter, and give him a peck on the cheek. "I'm sorry if that was awkward."

"Not at all. They're quite a lively bunch, aren't they?" He smiles at me and I let out a chuckle.

"You have no idea. The three of them could get a saint in trouble."

I decide I'm in no mood to clean up, so I leave it for another time.

"What time are you getting the van tomorrow?" I ask.

Peter shrugs. "Whenever I want. Perhaps I'll have a lie in to recover from tonight and then make up my mind," he jokes.

A good idea. Wish I didn't have to leave for work so early in the morning…

***

Ironically, last night's wish is sort of granted come Monday morning.

With tears still prickling in my eyes, I stare down at the half-crumpled letter in my pale hands. It's way too cold to be standing outside in the drizzle without a proper coat on, but I simply couldn't stand being inside the office any longer. As far as Mondays go, today has got to be the worst one ever.

"Hey, Claudia, are you okay?" Diane rushes up to me, putting her hand on my shoulder.

I know she got a letter too, but with better news than mine. For now. We're supposed to all be in the same boat, but it doesn't quite feel that way right now.

Rather than respond, I just sniffle and shrug.

"It sucks, hey. I hope they're at least paying you decently." Diane looks concerned, but I feel like her sympathy is mainly superficial. She'll be relieved that she's safe at the moment. I can't blame her, that was how I felt when I was spared during the last round of cost cutting.

"I just don't know what I'm going to do now, you

know? I suck at interviews," I complain.

She pats me on the back and gives me a wry smile. "It'll work out. At least you've got that man of yours to support you while you're looking."

Though I know she's just trying to make me feel better, her remark rubs me the wrong way.

"It's not like that, Diane," I grumble, wiping the remnants of tears away from the corner of my eye.

"Fine. I just meant at least you're not all on your own, you know?"

I shrug and decide to leave the topic before I say something I'll regret. Being told by the powers that be that my services are no longer required has really affected me. I'd underestimated how shit it would feel to no longer be needed.

Just when I turn away from Diane and start walking towards my regular spot, I realize that of course, the stupid car is still not fixed so I can't even go home on my own. Hopefully Peter is around and not yet in the middle of moving his things out of my garage.

With shaking fingers, I fish my phone out of my jeans pocket and dial his number. He answers almost immediately.

"Hi. Yeah, I'm really sorry to disturb, but could you come get me?" My voice trembles uncontrollably, and as soon as he says he's coming and cuts the phone, I'm crying again.

What a fucking mess.

I decide to hurry back inside to grab my coat which I'd left behind in my rush earlier, all the while doing my best not to look anyone in the eye. *With immediate effect,* they said. *Your services are no longer required with immediate effect.*

How worthless am I that they don't even need me to finish up my work, or do anything else? They've just discarded me in a meeting lasting about fifteen minutes. Bastards.

By the time I make my way back outside to wait for Peter, my anger and hurt has been largely replaced by detachment.

I don't even know how long I loiter around in the cold car until Peter arrives, but it must be quite a while because my fingernails have started turning purplish.

"Are you alright?" His voice makes an attempt at soothing me when he opens the passenger door for me, but I'm entirely too cold to warm up to him straight away.

"I'll survive," I snap as I sit down and shut the door.

"It doesn't take a genius to guess what's happened."

I shrug. It still hurts.

"Claudia," Peter says, resting his hand on my shoulder. "Look at me."

Despite not really wanting to, preferring to keep staring at my feet, I do finally turn my head to look in his direction. Almost immediately, the waterworks are back on and I start blubbering like crazy.

"With immediate effect. Can you believe that?" I cry.

He guides me into his arms, awkwardly, with the gear shift blocking the space between our seats. I rest my face on his shoulder and continue to complain. About the meeting, the HR woman who seemed to enjoy the whole thing, and mostly about how they couldn't wait to get me out of there.

"This is does not reflect on you, your abilities. You know that, right? These things aren't to be taken personally. It's all numbers. Profit and loss."

I want to believe his words, but my heart can't accept it right now, so the tears just keep on coming.

"But I've got to pay the car bill, and there's a leak in the roof, and..." I'm so overwhelmed, the words escape me. How am I going to manage?

I had wanted to save more, to be more organized, but something always happened that needed immediate attention. And it's not like my salary was all that much to begin with. But it was better than nothing at all.

"I'll understand if you don't want to share, but what package did they offer you?" he asks.

I shrug again, during the meeting they'd explained

it all, but everything had just gone in one ear and come out the other. I remember it must be in the letter, so I hand him the moist sheet of paper I've been clutching ever since coming out of the meeting.

He takes a moment to read through it, then gives it back to me.

"It's more than what they had to pay by law, that's decent of them. The way they've gone about it though..." Peter closes his other arm around me and kisses my hair. "They had no right to spring this on you without warning. Without giving you the chance to get used to the idea. You may have a case to sue them for not following proper procedure, if you want."

I shake my head, not suing anybody. It's best to just forget about it.

With his arms still around me, I close my eyes and try to focus on his touch, his soothing voice, but my throat feels like it's closing up and my chest is ready to explode. I don't know what I'm going to do now. While I've certainly made my fair share of mistakes in the past, I've always worked, never been in debt. I don't even know how one applies for benefits or what I'd be entitled to. What if I can't find another job soon enough and can't afford the upkeep on my house—Dad's house?

Frozen in place, with all these fears swirling in my mind, I don't know how much time passes. Neither am I in any state to keep track of where we are or where we're going. When Peter's car finally comes to a halt outside my house, I'm still in a state of shock.

"Let's get you inside," he says, but I don't move, until he walks around the car and opens the door for me, gesturing at me to get up. I follow him inside, largely on auto-pilot.

CHAPTER SIXTEEN

For the best part of Tuesday, I've been moping around the house with no real clue of what to do. I'd sat down with the laptop for a while, trying to update my CV, but just looking at it made me want to pull my hair out so I gave up. Looking at the Job Centre website didn't help any either.

I know I should do better, to get on track and start looking for a job as soon as possible, but somehow, everything still feels too raw, too painful. Part of me can't believe that this has actually happened to me.

"Any luck?" Peter asks, when he sees that I've put the laptop away again.

"Meh." I know I am being a complete bore, and terrible company, but I'm not ready to get out of my funk yet.

He's being a pretty good sport, holding off on his move in order to spend time with me while I'm down. And in return, I'm making things as difficult as I possibly can.

"You remember what you told me when we first met?" Peter sits down next to me and takes my hand. Despite this dark cloud hanging over my head, I still feel a hint of butterflies in my stomach at his touch.

"What's that?"

"That finding out about Stephanie and Chris was in a way a second chance. The same is the case for you now. A second chance to find out what you want to do in life."

The way he's caressing my hand is making me weak, as is the genuine look of concern on his face. I know I can be frustrating to be around, and when I get in a mood it's extremely hard for me to get back to normal, so I'm trying my best to let his words sink in.

"I guess so."

"Think about it. When you were little, did you dream of working in a call centre? Probably not. What *did* you want to do?"

I shrug. I know what I wanted to do, for as long as I can remember, but there's no way that will turn out well. Just look how Dad ended up.

"Paint, I guess."

"So paint. The money they gave you is tax free, the whole point is that you use it to cover costs while you figure out your next move."

"Yeah, but why take risks with it, when I already know I'll need a job by the end of it all anyway?"

"Says who? I've seen your work, that seascape you gave me for my new place is nothing short of a masterpiece."

Although I should feel flattered, hearing such big words thrown around for something I cobbled together in a few hours grates me the wrong way. He's bullshitting me. I take my hand out from under his grasp and fold my arms.

"Show me one guidance counselor who will advise someone to pursue painting as a career. One. One responsible parent, who thinks their child should play with acrylics and oil all day, instead of study something sensible like accounting." I'm trying hard not to let my annoyance shine through in my tone, but I'm failing miserably. My heart is hammering in my throat and I can't help but go on the defensive. He's delusional if he thinks becoming an artist is a good career choice. Where else did the term 'starving artist' originate from, if not the cold, hard reality? Even if you don't end up broke, you'll end up alone.

"All I'm saying is, there's no harm in trying it out. I could pick up the phone right now and get you a few sales immediately, based on just that painting you gave me. You could exhibit, or even do commissioned work."

I shake my head, what does it prove that he knows people with more money than sense who would buy some unknown person's paintings, just on his say-so? Nothing. It proves absolutely nothing.

"Fine. Let's not argue."

"Think about it."

Despite still being grumpy about the turn our conversation has taken, I decide to keep quiet and let him have the last word. Just at that moment, my phone rings and I jump up to get it.

"Hello?"

"Hi, Bob here. About your car," the voice on the other end says. The chat that follows does absolutely nothing to improve my mood. After waiting for some part for over a week, they've now figured out that it doesn't actually fix the problem. They're going to have to open up the engine.

"I don't think it's cost-effective, to be honest," Bob finally says. "You'd be better off looking at something newer."

"Alright." I take a deep breath in an attempt to get my frustration under control. "I'll think about it and call you back later."

"Not a problem. Have a good weekend." The line goes dead and yet I'm still standing there, clutching the phone. It never rains but it pours.

"What's wrong?" Peter asks.

"Apparently the work is going to cost a lot more than expected. More than the car is worth."

I feel defeated and sink back into the sofa, covering my face with my hands. *Great.* I guess it's time to start looking at classified ads for a new car. There goes most of my redundancy payment.

"Tell you what, why don't we go for a drive?" Peter suggests.

I shrug. Why not? Staying here sure isn't going to

improve matters.

"Where to?"

"Does it matter, no matter where you go, it's nice around here. And it looks like the rain has stopped too."

He makes an excellent point.

***

I stare blankly out of the passenger window, watching the shrubs, trees and fields zip past while Peter navigates around the quaint country lanes. Everything is glistening in the hazy sunlight that is trying to break through the clouds. Usually, drives make me happy, because there's always something to see. City life has never appealed to me, too much concrete tends to make me feel claustrophobic.

Today though, even the rich colors of autumn do nothing to inspire me or cheer me up. We continue on in silence, until I notice we're leaving the scenic countryside and entering a town. I'm about to ask where we're going, when Peter pulls up outside a big, sprawling used car dealership.

Oh God, he's not actually doing this now?

"Just go with it," he says, noticing my horrified expression.

"U-huh."

He gets out, then walks around and opens the

door for me like the gentleman he is, and guides me towards the main entrance of the showroom. The large parking area is full of cars of varying sizes, colors and brands.

"Don't you think I should do some research first?" I whisper, while pulling at his arm to convince him to turn back before the slick salesman notices us.

"Why? Anything you need to know is right here." Peter pats his pocket where he keeps his smart phone.

I take a look around at the small cars parked towards the left of the lot, and quickly notice they haven't got anything over five years old. Great. Not only am I completely unprepared, I'm also in no position to even consider any of these cars.

"How can I help you?" The salesman rushes up to us, and shakes Peter's hand.

"We're looking for a hatchback, low miles, good fuel efficiency. Rest is up to her."

"Very good, sir. How about this Ford Fiesta?" We are led up to a lime green car parked right outside the office. Seeing the price tag makes me want to turn and run immediately.

"That looks quite nice, doesn't it, Claudia? It's practically new." Peter leans over to read the information card on the windscreen more carefully, while I try to tug him in the opposite direction.

All I can do is shake my head.

"Can we have a moment, please?" I ask the sales

guy, who holds up his hands in sort of a defeated gesture and nods.

As soon as he's out of earshot, I turn to Peter. "You've seen how much they paid me. I can't afford any of these cars!"

"You don't have to. Let me help out."

His answer is exactly what I was afraid of. This is not fucking happening.

"I'm not letting you buy it for me!"

"And why not?"

"Because…" My breath has started going ragged, despite the drive to get there, and all my attempts to get my negativity under control, I'm pissed off all over again. "It feels icky."

"Me doing something nice for you, so you can focus on whatever it is you want to do—whether that's painting or finding a new job—without worrying about maintaining an unreliable, not to mention unsafe old car, feels *icky?*"

Part of me realizes how stupid that sounds, but it's the honest truth. The thought of having Peter spend thousands of pounds on a car for me does feel wrong. I can't accept it. I wouldn't know how to ever repay him, except actually returning the money. The niggle is, I would not spend so much on a vehicle. He's forcing me into something I would never do myself even if I did have enough money in the bank.

"At least you could have asked me before just

bringing me here. I just found out about the bloody car an hour ago!"

"It wasn't exactly pre-planned. While driving around, I kept thinking about how to cheer you up and thought maybe solving at least one of your problems might do the job."

"Well, it's not working." I fold my arms and glare at him. The fact that he still looks amused, as though I'm the unreasonable one, is making my annoyance turn to anger.

"At least you won't have to worry about transport."

"Instead I'd be worrying about you spending all that money on me. Seriously. Buying me an expensive outfit was pushing it, but a car crosses way too many boundaries. I'm just not comfortable with this. You throwing money around is not going to cheer me up." And especially not while he also doesn't have a job either. It's not just irresponsible, it's plain stupid.

"Fine." Peter takes a deep breath and holds up his hands in defeat. "I just wanted to help. Forget about it then."

Although I'm still trembling with all sorts of emotions, I do my best to swallow it all. He was just trying to help, I can see that. It's just so frustrating that with him, *helping out* quickly turns into trying to push me into seeing things his way. I need a new car, that much is certain, but I can't buy it like this.

BEAUTIFUL STRANGER

"Fine." I ignore the salesman who is eyeing us curiously from across the lot as we return to Peter's car.

"Can I at least take you out for dinner tonight, to make up for all this?" Peter asks, while pulling out of the parking lot and joining the main road.

"Sure. That would be nice," I say, but my tone doesn't reflect my words.

We drive around aimlessly for a little while longer, before making a quick stop at his new place. Always the efficient one, he somehow managed to get some of his post forwarded already so there are a few letters for him to pick up. Rather than head to my place, we go for a short walk around Windsor town centre, which despite the chill in the air is busy as ever.

Now that office hours are over, the town is full of tourists and locals alike, most of whom are congregating around the castle. Looking at the imposing facade which towers over the little shops next to it, I can't blame them. It looks magnificent against the dramatic cloud cover behind it.

Sensing the change in my demeanor, Peter takes my hand as we stand there, opposite the massive stone structure, just staring at it.

"Beautiful, isn't it. So much history in those walls," I remark.

He nods, then pulls me closer against him with his arm around me.

"I'm sorry about earlier, Claudia. I should've known to ask you first."

"That's okay. I'm sorry for overreacting." I tiptoe slightly and give him a peck on the cheek. "Ever since yesterday, I just don't have my head on straight."

"What do you say, we have a pint at The King and Castle, then think about dinner. I know a great little Italian just a short walk from here," he suggests.

I shoot him a smile, keen to shake off the negativity from before. "That sounds great."

CHAPTER SEVENTEEN

The next day, I wake up bright and early despite having nowhere to go and nothing to do. No job, and still no prospects. Peter is already up by the looks of it so I put on a warm robe and head to the kitchen, seeing what he's up to.

As usual, he's made a pot of tea and is settled on the couch with the paper.

"Morning." He looks up and smiles at me as I enter. "Tea?"

"Yes please." I plop down next to him and watch as he pours it for me in the extra mug he's already put out. I'm going to miss this when he moves into his new place.

I lift the cup to my lips, about to take the first sip when I notice a pad with some notes on the table.

"Working on something?" I ask.

Peter shrugs, and smiles mysteriously. "Just a few ideas. For my *new and exciting life.*"

"I see." I settle back into the cushions, waiting for further clarifications, but he keeps quiet. Perhaps he's not ready to share his conclusions yet.

"What did you have planned for today?" he asks finally, after scribbling down one last thought and putting the pad into his laptop bag.

"Nothing. I don't know." Even though I've had time to let my new circumstances sink in a little bit, as well as a good night's rest, it still hurts. I'm not ready to start the job hunt yet, the thought makes my stomach turn.

"Well, it's no use to sit around wallowing in self-pity all day. How about we go do something. A walk, maybe? It's unseasonably warm today."

I know he's right. Despite the rocky start we got off to yesterday, it was nice to get out of the house.

"Walk where?" I ask, adding up the local options in my head. It's too late in the year to visit gardens, but there are plenty of parks to choose from.

"What's nearest?"

"Virginia Water? The parking is practically opposite where we first met."

"Brilliant. I'll be ready when you are."

Within half an hour, I'm showered and dressed for the occasion in sturdy leather boots and warm clothes. It may be a sunny day and warm for the time of year, but it's still November. Peter is indeed ready as well, though his attire is a lot less cautious.

"You sure you're not going to get cold?" I ask, pointing at the light jacket he plans on carrying.

"I was thinking we could go for a little jog, in which case no, this should be more than sufficient."

A jog. That prospect makes our little outing a lot less exciting, but I don't argue. If that's what he wants, I'll give it a go. I guess jogging is how he stays in shape, and I certainly can't argue with the end result of all that hard work. My gentle curves do not require that kind of maintenance.

The drive is predictably short, and the parking lot is empty, as one would expect from a weekday in late autumn. Soon after we park up, Peter starts stretching his arms and legs, preparing for that jog, and I just clumsily stand around watching him.

"Let's start slow, so you can keep up," he suggests.

I shrug. "I guess. Let's see how it goes."

My non-committal response makes him smile. I'm sure he won't have much to smile about once he realizes that I'm about as fit as a sloth. Jogging is so not my thing.

We start at a very slow pace up the pathway leading away from the parking and towards the lake shore. It's quiet, almost desolately empty, allowing me to really take in the understated beauty of the place. I love Virginia Water because it looks deceptively natural despite being man-made centuries ago.

While I'm distracted looking at the reflections of the turned leaves in the calm waters of the lake, I slow, while Peter keeps up the same pace as before, the gap between us widening with every step.

I try to catch up, but am held back by my ever intensifying breaths. *Ugh, I hate jogging.* Why can't we just go for a walk, so at least we have the opportunity to look at the place without risking falling over our own feet.

"Wait up," I say, waving at him when he finally looks back at where I am.

I run up to him and lean with both hands on my knees.

"This is a lovely place, I'm glad you suggested it," Peter says.

"Yeah…" I gasp for air a few times, unable to finish my sentence.

"How about we walk slowly for a bit, and then continue?" he suggests.

I want to suggest that we just walk throughout, but keep quiet, opting instead to conserve my breath.

After a few minutes, he asks if I'm ready and I nod, ignoring my better judgment. We start off again, and I make it about three hundred yards, before I'm totally shattered. Peter has barely broken a sweat.

"Go on without me!" I exclaim dramatically.

"No way, what's the fun in that?"

"Really. I'll only slow you down." I shake out my cramped limbs and open up my warm coat, which is making me feel like I'm suffocating.

"Just a little more, we've hardly covered any distance yet!"

I look back at the path we've just come off, noting that the turn off to the parking has since disappeared in the distance. It looks bloody far away enough for me!

"That's like half a mile right there!" I protest.

"So?"

"Enough jogging, honestly. Let's just walk, what do you say?"

"You give up too easily," Peter says, playfully patting me on my arm.

What is meant as encouragement only pisses me off though.

"Just like with my painting, huh?" I remark, yesterday's arguments still ringing in my ears.

"Right." He pauses, scrutinizing me for a moment. "If you don't push past your comfort zone, you'll stagnate."

"What if I'm content? If it's not broken, don't fix it?" My face is burning up, partially from the jogging just now, but mainly because I'm angry again.

"You don't look content." Peter's face has tensed up too. This isn't just about jogging anymore.

"That's because I hate jogging. I only agreed to it to do you a favor, but I fucking hate it."

"Whatever. If you want to walk, let's walk." He turns away from me, heading further up the path around the lake.

"No. Let's have it out here once and for all." I put my hands on my hips and wait. "Best we sort this out now."

"Fine. What is it you want to say?" he asks,

pausing again with his head turned back my way.

"You tell me? You're the one who seems to disapprove of everything I do, from my career choices to what kind of car I want to drive."

"You have so much potential, so much talent. Instead you'd much rather waste away in a job you hate because it feels safe. Well, it wasn't. They threw you out. And still you want to keep your head in the sand and go right back and replace it with another dead end job."

His words hurt. They did throw me out, like I'm worthless. Way to go rubbing that in.

"It's a job. You go there to earn money, that's the only use it has. Life isn't all unicorns and rainbows, you know!"

"Believe me, I know. And I've seen more of it than you have."

Great, now he deals the age card. *I know better because I'm older than you.* How fucking original.

"You don't seem to act like it. You've gone and quit a well-paying job in order to *'figure out what you want to do with your life'.*Puh-lease! You know what that sort of thing is called in the real world? A midlife crisis!"

Although he had sort of kept his composure so far, my last remark sends him over the edge too.

"Oh yeah? I've paid my dues, made my fair share of mistakes; fifteen years' worth. But rather than listening to my advice, you're stubbornly on your way to doing the same thing. Take it from me, you waste the opportunities you have when you're still young, while you don't yet have anyone depending on you, you will regret it eventually!"

"At least I will be responsible for doing something I regret, rather than jumping head first into a stupid fantasy on somebody else's say-so!"

We're both breathing heavily from our shouting match, and still glaring at one another.

"I don't think this is going to work. Best I go home," I say through gritted teeth, and look back where we had just come from.

"If that's what you want."

"Yeah, it's what I want. You go and jog all you want, I'll walk."

"Right. Your choice." He turns as well but doesn't move.

Still fuming, I don't see a way out except through. There is no backing down now. This isn't working for me. *We* are not going to work. After walking a few steps, I pause and look back once.

"Move out your stuff as soon as possible. I'm going to need the space."

For a split second, our eyes meet, and I think I see surprise in his expression. Whatever. I'm done with being told what to do and how to think. It's been nice believing in our little romance, but I'm not ready to jump down his crazy rabbit holes with him.

I want a stable new job, a sensible new-to-me car, and a predictable, organized life. My days of impulsively leaving the real world behind to go off on some adventure are over. If he can't understand that then it's his loss.

I march back towards the car, out of the parking lot and down the main road that leads to my house. It takes me twenty minutes at the determined pace I'm going at, by the end of which I'm again out of breath and feeling more lost than I had been before.

Had I really meant it? Yes. We're too different, too set on our different paths.

With shaking fingers, I turn on the kettle and deposit a teabag in my mug. No need to make a pot full, not if it's just me drinking it. As the water starts to boil, silent tears start to run down my cheeks.

In the heat of the moment, I'd finally snapped and let my doubts run rampant. That whole debacle at the racecourse should have taught me something. I should have known then that it wouldn't work. One the one hand he seems to think money can buy happiness, on the other hand he recklessly wants to spend it until there is none left.

Just liking someone isn't enough. Compatibility in the bedroom means nothing outside of it. Not when you're going in opposite directions.

Peter reaches my place about an hour after me,

letting himself in with the key I'd given him. I'd just finished packing his things into a large overnight bag five minutes earlier. My house is once more my own.

"Can we talk?" he calls out, knocking on my bedroom where I've hidden myself away as soon as I heard the car enter the drive.

"What's the point?" I sigh, turning over and pressing my tear-stained faced into the other pillow on my bed. It has his scent in it, causing a fresh lump in my throat. Lurking around in here while he leaves is no way to end things, I know that. It would be hypocritical to accuse him of being immature and then refuse to face him in the end. And so I fight all my instincts and get out of bed, drying my face and smoothing my hair down until I feel halfway presentable.

He's waiting right outside when I open the bedroom door.

"Are you sure this is what you want?" he asks, his face hard and eyes stone cold.

I nod, while biting my lip, glancing at the floor. It's what's right. What's best for both of us.

"I can't change on a dime, neither should you. I hope you find what you're looking for." My words sound forced, that's how much effort it takes for me to speak quietly rather than scream out, releasing all the heartache I feel.

"Your keys." He hands me the spare bunch, his

fingers brushing past my palm, making me flinch. My heart is telling me to ask him to stay, but I don't give in.

Although I fear the look in his eyes, I force myself to look into them one last time.

"Goodbye, Peter."

He nods and turns on his heel. "I'll empty the shed tomorrow. Unless you change your mind."

Somehow, I don't think I will.

CHAPTER EIGHTEEN

Every day I wake up, and for a moment I expect that the bed next to me will still be slightly warm, but it's not. It's cold. The pillow is unused. There is no pot of tea waiting for me in the living room. All I have to look forward to is an empty house and the occasional phone call from Mom, or Alice, calling to check how I am.

I've lost track of the amount of tears I've shed, before reaching the kind of blank emptiness I find myself in now. The pain has dulled, though it hasn't gone away. I miss him, desperately so.

When Peter packed up all his things last week I felt like it was goodbye forever. I would never see him again. Every day I'm fighting the urge to phone him, to ask him to come back. So far I haven't caved.

It's for the best. We're not compatible. Mom was right, I do have a strange talent for dating irresponsible men. Peter was supposed to be different, more mature. As it turns out, looks deceive. He was just like all the others: impulsive, irrational and reckless with his finances. And rather than listen to reason, he wanted me to jump into the deep end with him.

It would have never worked out. He wanted to go

off and travel the world, while I try to make it as an artist. In the real world that's just not feasible.

People need jobs to pay bills. Jobs that have nothing to do with what we dreamed of doing when we were kids. Real jobs aren't fun, they're so dull nobody would ever do them if it wasn't for the pay check. Anyone who thinks otherwise is deluding themselves.

Over the past few days, I'd worked out the bare miniMom I would need a month for my daily expenses, I've also calculated I can afford to spend about a grand on a new car if I want to keep a three-month buffer. It's time I took my job hunt more seriously. Three months of living on savings is not a safety net, it's panic-inducing.

Once out of bed, I reluctantly go into the kitchen. So empty. While I haven't sorted out my car troubles, I'll need to have groceries delivered. Even the one pound ninety-nine they charge for delivery hurts, so I've been putting off my first order. My cupboards and fridge are getting empty pretty fast, while I do my best and eat my way through forgotten cans of soup and other random pantry staples everyone inevitably collects over the years.

I'll order groceries when I've exhausted all other options, I tell myself while pouring boiling water over a teabag containing some strange herbal concoction I found in the back of a cupboard when my normal tea had finished. Luckily it doesn't require milk, because I'm out of that too.

At least twenty applications today. That's my goal. Then I'll head into the shed and finish my latest work-in-progress as a reward. It's amazing how productive I've been these last few days, despite everything.

Just when I've finished my first cup and am debating whether I can face the laptop without a second one, I hear the post drop through the front door. More bills, no doubt... Might as well check that first before starting on my first of many applications.

The collection of envelopes on my welcome mat looks mostly predictable. Brown envelope: Council Tax, white envelope with bar code: credit card bill. However, underneath it all there is one which doesn't look familiar at all. Thick, expensive-looking paper with a gold logo on top which I do not recognize. *Galleria Eclectica* written in an ornate font. My first thought is that it must be an ad for something, though unusually it's addressed rather formally to me; *Ms. De Wit,* no first name.

I open it and start reading.

Dear Ms. De Wit,

We are excited to announce the grand opening of our new venue in Windsor on Saturday, the 10th of December, 3 pm onwards; address below. You are cordially invited to attend, though we hope for more involvement from your side.

As you may imagine, a lot of planning has gone into the launch of a brand new art gallery, including booking an impressive line-up of artists for our first showcase, 'Visions of Berkshire'. Unfortunately due to unforeseen events, we still find ourselves with a few open spots. Having had the pleasure of inspecting one of your works in person, as well as seeing photographs of your portfolio, we feel that you would be a perfect fit for our event.

The exhibition is a showcase as well as a sales opportunity for up and coming artists in the Windsor region, and we are confident it will be a great opportunity for your work to gain more exposure. We hope that you will consider this chance— despite the short notice—and get in touch by the 1st of December with a shortlist of five possible exhibits (large canvases, spec enclosed), if you wish to participate.

Our terms are very attractive—20% commission for any sales inspired by our event—no hidden charges and complimentary appraisal service.

Yours faithfully,
Lauren Clackton
Proprietor Galleria Eclectica

BEAUTIFUL STRANGER

What the hell? This Lauren person has seen my work in person as well as some photographs? But I haven't displayed it anywhere, nor have I ever catalogued my old paintings… *Peter!* He said he'd taken a look inside my studio-cum-shed. It's the only explanation. Plus he's the only person who actually has one of my paintings, Mom excluded.

I'm not sure whether to feel flattered, or as if my privacy has been invaded. Still conflicted, I fold the letter and pop it back in its envelope. How do I even know this is a respectable gallery? And their terms… twenty per cent does sound reasonable, but how do I know whether that's attractive without knowing the market rates?

And then there's the matter of whether I *want* a bunch of random strangers to critique my paintings over bubbly and finger food?

Forget it, I don't have time for this nonsense. I throw the letter back on the pile of bills on the side table in the hall and settle down with the laptop, fully committed to not letting anything drag me off task. I have jobs to apply for, which will make me actual money. Letters promising me eighty per cent of some fictional amount in case someone, somewhere likes something I painted are just not going to do the trick.

Scrolling through ad after ad, from telesales to phone surveys, I can almost feel my will to live escape me. These are all easy jobs, things I'm more than qualified for, but every single one of them already has fifty or so applicants fighting over it, making it seem like I'll never be able to compete.

Still, I soldier on and manage ten applications with custom-written cover notes by lunchtime. That's when the doorbell rings.

I get up, rubbing my aching shoulders on the way to check who it could be, only to be greeted by Mom's face, peeking in through the little window in the front door.

"Hey, darling, how are you doing?" she exclaims when I open up. "I thought I'd check in on you…"

She gives me a warm hug and invites herself in.

"Hi, Mom."

"Wow, it's cold outside. Let's make a cup of coffee, what do you say?" She seems to talk mainly to herself while unraveling herself from layers of warm clothes, mufflers, even earmuffs. As usual for this season, Mom is dressed to survive an Arctic storm, rather than the mildly wintery temperatures we're seeing today.

"I'm out of coffee," I remark, as she piles the discarded garments into my arms.

"A cup of coffee is just what I need right now. Wait, what?"

I give her an apologetic look which does nothing to soothe her disappointment.

"Herbal tea?" I suggest.

BEAUTIFUL STRANGER

"Claudia! That's no way to greet your mother. No coffee, at all?"

She shakes her head as she opens my kitchen cupboards, rifling through their sparse contents.

"Really, it's a good thing I came by, you seem to be starving yourself."

"Just haven't had the chance to shop while I don't have a car..." I try to justify myself, though I know she's right. I should have ordered food by now. One can only eat so many lunches and dinners consisting of random cans of oxtail soup.

"Anyway, this won't do. Let's go out, my treat." One by one, she picks up her warm clothes and puts them back on. "Go on, get dressed! We're going out for lunch."

I look down at my shabby old pajama pants and paint-splattered fluffy slippers. Ugh.

"I don't really feel like—"

"Nonsense! Look at you, you're turning into a recluse all by yourself!"

Funny, I've been by myself long enough but she's never had this complaint before. I swallow my protests and head into the bedroom to find something to wear. Laundry is also well overdue so my choices are severely limited. Finally I settle on a Fair Isle pattern knitted sweater and some jeans, the only ones that are still somewhat clean.

"Come on, let's go," she commands, while

clapping her hands as if I'm ten years old, attempting to herd me out the door and into her car. I grudgingly do as she says.

On the way out, she pauses a few steps behind me.

"Claudia, what's this?" I turn to find her waving the envelope with the gold lettering at me. Damn, I'd totally forgotten about that.

"Nothing. Just some bullshit letter."

"No really, what is it? The logo looks familiar." She opens it and peeks inside, before fishing the letter out with her carefully manicured fingers.

"Don't," I sigh, knowing it's impossible to discourage her when she's set her mind on something. She wants to know what it is, and she's hell-bent on finding out.

"This…" She points at the paper, her eyes flitting back and forth as she's reading through more of it. "This is wonderful, Claudia! Congratulations!"

"I suppose."

"You *are* going to do it, right? It would be wonderful for your work to be seen by more people."

"I hadn't quite thought about it." As soon as I finish my sentence, Mom gives me a disapproving look.

"Whatever. We're going for lunch now and you can tell me all about it on the way."

After more initial prodding and probing, I finally tell her the whole story. About the painting I'd given

Peter, and my educated guess that he's behind all this. By the time I finish, we've reached the restaurant and are stationary in the parking lot.

"Remind me why you two broke up?" she asks after listening to everything.

"Because he's just like all the others. Irresponsible. It couldn't have worked out, we're way too different."

"Oh, Claudia." She reaches over and squeezes my hand while giving me a wry smile. "Sometimes different is just what you need."

"I disagree." I fold my arms and stare straight out the windscreen at the white wall surrounding the parking lot. "Plus, isn't this exactly the thing that drove you and Dad apart? Him living in his dream world, fantasizing about breaking out as an artist, and you stuck in reality trying to make ends meet?"

"Darling, there's nothing wrong with dreaming."

"But, Dad…"

"Your dad knew what he wanted, I must give him credit for that. The issue wasn't with his career choice, it was that he was so absorbed by his work that there was no space for *my* dreams, my goals in our marriage."

I consider her words for a moment, trying to apply them to my own situation.

"What are you trying to say?" I ask.

"This man, Peter, he was trying to support *you*. Help you achieve *your* goals. That's a rare quality in men. Most of them only have eyes for what they want to achieve themselves."

"But what about money? What if I'm not good enough?"

Tears are prickling in my eyes now, after days of trying to swallow my hurt.

"Only one way of finding out. You can always look for a job later, can't you?"

"I made a mistake, haven't I?" I whisper.

She puts her arm around my shoulder, letting me rest my head against her.

"Only you can decide that. All I'm saying is, you could do a lot worse than having a man who would go this far to help you reach your goals."

"So you think I should exhibit at that gallery opening thing?"

"Opportunities like that don't come along every day."

"I don't know they're even legit," I argue.

"They've been in the paper, apparently it's quite a prestigious thing and that Clackton woman used to curate at the Tate Modern." She gives me a pat on my shoulder, before opening her door. "Let's go now, I really need a coffee before lunch."

No wonder she was so excited about the letter. The Tate Modern, wow. This new bit of information has the potential to change everything. Could it be that Peter's comments about my paintings were more than just flattery? Could his remarks have been more educated and sensible than I'd given him credit for?

Throughout lunch, I try to make sense of all she's said, and whatever my heart is trying to tell me. I *have* made a massive mistake. I just hope it's not too late to set things right.

CHAPTER NINETEEN

After having lunch, Mom insists we buy groceries as well and so she drops me off back home with enough food to feed an army. While I wave her goodbye, I keep eyeing the letter on the side table in the hall.

I'd never really thought about exhibiting my work, I've always lacked the confidence. Could I have been selling myself short like Peter said?

Peter… Clearly he must have set this up before our big fight, so would it be rude to accept the offer anyway? Mom didn't seem to think so, but then she probably thinks I still have a chance to make things right with him.

I'm not so sure now, I've said some pretty mean things and done a brilliant job of convincing myself I'd made the right call. Now, a week later, what if he's moved on? *Only one way to find out,* as Mom said.

Staring at his picture on my phone, I hover over his number. I should call him. Apologize. Talk things through.

Or should I call that gallery place first to set up a meeting? They wanted five large paintings, I have maybe three or four which I'm proud of, the rest are too old, too small, too crappy… No, I shouldn't meet with them until I'm prepared.

BEAUTIFUL STRANGER

I hit dial before my better sense prevails and wait with bated breath for the dial tone. It rings, once, twice, then clicks and I forget to breathe when I hear his voice.

"Hello?"

My heart is hammering in my throat, and I don't know what to say. He must hate me, he absolutely must.

"Claudia?"

Shit, shit, shit!

"Hi," my voice trembles. "I'm so very sorry." Before I can catch myself, tears start to flow and I'm sobbing on the phone. It occurs to me I'm embarrassing myself, but I don't care.

"Calm down, what happened?" Peter says. So calm, so warm. Like he genuinely cares.

"Nothing! Nothing happened. I'm an idiot, I made a mistake and I'm so sorry," I cry.

"Let's talk in person, what do you say? I can be at your place in fifteen minutes."

I nod, forgetting he can't see me, then swallow hard, so at least I can get a proper response out.

"Okay. Thanks."

He hangs up, and I'm left holding the phone, wondering if I am actually losing my mind and imagining everything that just happened. Surely, after I've been so horrible to him, essentially kicking him out of my house, he didn't just agree to come over at the drop of a hat, just because I called? That makes no sense at all.

Minute after minute passes while I continue try to work it out in my head. What am I going to say when he gets here? And the place looks like a war zone, I should probably clean up. Just when I get up to put the groceries away, his car pulls up outside and I leave everything exactly where it is to open the door.

"Hi!" I wipe my face with the back of my hand, and shuffle back and forth from one leg to the other while he walks up.

"Hi." He looks into my eyes, making my knees tremble uncontrollably.

His expression is calm, like he's unaffected at all by the turmoil I'm feeling.

"I wanted to say…" I stammer, then realize we're still standing in the doorway, so I step aside to let him in.

"Yes?"

"I wanted to apologize for being so horrible to you. I'll understand if you don't forgive me, but I had to say sorry." I blink a few times, trying to ward off further tears, but my eyes well up again anyway.

"I must say, it was rather unexpected."

I avert my gaze, staring at my feet. Mismatched socks? Really? Oh my God, this is getting worse and worse.

"Love what you've done with the place," Peter

remarks dryly, as he walks through to the living room. There are papers, sketches, half-finished drawings and random magazine clippings everywhere. I really should have thought this through and tidied up.

"I guess despite all my protests, I've done what you said. Painted."

He turns to face me, the beginnings of a smile on his face.

"And?"

"I got that letter this morning."

"Ah yes, the letter. Of course." He picks up the nearest sketch from the coffee table and sits down on the couch, studying it carefully. It's another concept for a landscape/human figure mash-up similar to the painting I'd given him for his new place.

"I realize nothing I can say will justify what I did, but…" I pause when he picks up another scrap of paper, a drawing I'd shaded in with watercolor pencil.

"Go on," he says.

"Losing my job was pretty much the worst thing that's ever happened to me, except for when I got the news about Dad, of course."

"I understand that."

"And then the car, and everything, and I wasn't ready to hear what you—or anyone for that matter—said to me. I've only ever shown my work to family before, because I didn't think it was good enough. But you're right. I should at least give it a shot."

"I shouldn't have pushed you, but given you time to get used to your new situation first. I tried to rush you, and for that I'm sorry."

"And this past week has been hell. I've missed you so much."

"Evidently." He gestures at the chaos surrounding us.

"But if it's too late, I totally understand."

"Too late? Claudia, I waited fifteen years to finally meet someone like you, someone who would challenge me rather than just take my credit card and ignore my very existence otherwise. It's never too late." He turns to me, his eyes burning into mine so intensely it takes my breath away again.

"I'm sorry for all the things I said."

"You weren't all wrong. I'm sorry I tried to force my opinions on you."

We share a smile.

"I missed you too, Claudia. More than I can express. If we can get past our differences, I promise I'll do better."

"Me too." I scoot closer to him, sighing deeply when his arms finally surround me. This is exactly what I needed. "I think I love you."

"I love you too."

We gaze into each other's eyes for a blissful few seconds. Both at ease, both reassured by what we see.

"I'm still not going to let you buy me a car

though!" I remark.

"We're going to have to work on that," he jokes.

He leans into me, our lips connecting finally in a kiss so intense it feels like fireworks are ready to erupt from my chest. I can't suppress a sob, making him pause.

"I thought I'd lost you," I explain.

"I'd been waiting for you," he responds.

"Why didn't you call me? Try to make me change my mind?"

"If there's one thing I learned in the past, it's that you can't *make* women do anything, least of all change their minds, unless that's what they want themselves."

He talks sense. I had to get to this conclusion myself or I would have just pushed him away all over again.

I'm overcome with a grave need for him, for his affection, his love. But before we get too distracted, there's something else that needs clearing up.

"That letter, how did you manage it?" I ask, though suddenly uncertain I want the answer.

"Lauren is an old friend, from university. After nosing around in your shed, I couldn't help myself and asked for her opinion. Whether it would be commercially viable. She was so taken with what I'd shown her that she wanted to invite you to join the exhibition. Actually, I had very little to do with it."

His modesty makes me smile. Sure, *very*

little, except he orchestrated the whole thing.

"I should mention that I do also have a stake in her business, just as a silent partner. I don't have any decision-making powers, and she wouldn't listen to me even if I did."

I pull back, and stare at him with my mouth half open in surprise.

"You're what?"

"She approached me last year, when she was just drawing up the plans for her business, so I put her in contact with the venture capital division at the firm. Then when we got talking about your work she mentioned her investor wanted out, so I bought his share. After ensuring it was a sound investment, of course. Just because I don't want to work at an investment bank anymore doesn't mean I can't use my experience and knowledge for some personal investments." Peter smiles.

No way! Not only is he friends with a seemingly influential figure in the modern art world, he's also part owner of a chain of galleries? How much money *does* he have exactly? I suspect I don't really want to know the answer to that, it would only freak me out.

"Why didn't you say something?"

"We only finalized the paperwork this past week, there was nothing to tell yet."

The way he's looking at me, with such tenderness

in his eyes, convinces me. I believe him. I guess that's what all the mysterious note-taking was all about last week. The whole thing is strangely funny. I panic because he wants to buy me a car, when at the same time he thinks nothing of buying part of a business to help out a friend.

"What's funny?"

I shake my head, but can't wipe the grin off my face. Oh my God, this whole situation is too surreal. "Nothing. Kiss me again."

He smiles back at me and gives me a wink. "That, I can do."

Before I know it, I'm on my back and he's on all fours above me, his lips pressed tightly into mine. Our tongues dance around one another, not to tease but to seduce. We're hungry, starved for affection, as our rushed movements clearly demonstrate.

He peels my clothes off in a hurry, while I struggle with his until he helps out. My hands once again roam his perfect body, the sculpted muscles which I know to hold so much strength. He's already hard, has been probably since the first make-up kiss. I love the effect my body seems to have on him.

With his elbows resting either side of my head, he lowers himself onto me, our bodies pressed together impatiently, aching to merge fully.

Then, without warning, he lifts himself and takes my hand, pulling me up with him. He rushes into the bedroom, his hand still clutching my wrist so I can do nothing but run along behind him. Not that I had other plans, no. The bedroom will be just fine.

We all but tear the remainder of our clothes off and leave them dumped on the carpet. He lies down on his back, gesturing at me to climb on top.

"Ride me," he demands.

I bite my lip in anticipation as I straddle him, guiding his length towards my entrance in a feverish attempt to find sweet salvation. The way he looks at me makes me forget myself. There's so much need in his eyes, yet so much tenderness as well. I don't doubt he truly cares about me, he truly wants to see me succeed at whatever I choose to do. Why didn't I see that before?

He bucks his hips, dragging me out of my trance. When I lower myself onto him, a gasp escapes my lips and my eyes snap shut. It feels so good, so right to be so close to him. To once again let our bodies become one.

As I start to move my hips, grinding into him for more pleasure, he does too and soon our bodies find a common rhythm. Like waves in the sea, we rock forward, tensions mounting until the end is almost in sight, then pulling back to make the moment last longer.

Things feel different, this time around. There is still that undeniable passion we feel for one another, that desperate yearning to give pleasure as well as receive. But there's also a deeper connection that I don't think was there before.

He reaches out for my hands, wrapping his fingers around mine, allowing me to lean on him while speeding up. I continue to ride him, while staying completely focused on his face. I missed falling asleep next to him, his arm protectively around me, making me feel safe. And I missed this expression so much, the calm before his release.

Time seems to slow while I speed up. A slow burn develops in my thigh muscles, but I'm not so easily discouraged. Underneath me, his muscular body starts to glisten in the dim ambient light. He's so beautiful, so perfect, groans of pleasure escaping his lips with every thrust.

Unlike other times we've made love, gone is the illusion of control from his movements, his eyes are shut now, their brilliant depths hidden for the time being as I push him towards the limits of control.

I know now that although things might not always be easy, it's worth fighting for. In one last ditch effort, I push on, focused entirely on him, every slight change in expression, the subtle tremble of his lower lip that signals I'm on the right track.

As he erupts, so do I. Our bodies come to a halt when we're at our closest. His arms wrap around me, forcing me into a tight embrace.

We stay put, me on top of him cradled in his arms, until our breaths slow down to normal and even the last trace of stickiness evaporates off our skin.

"Will you stay the night?" I ask.

"One condition," Peter responds.

"What's that?"

"Tomorrow we stay at my place. I even have a bed now."

I smile into his chest before kissing him right in the centre of it. "Fair enough."

EPILOGUE

My heart is beating so hard, I feel like it might try to burst through my chest. What if people don't like my work? What if it turns out to be a huge failure?

Sure, Lauren seemed to like what she saw when I brought my five canvases in last week, but what if she's wrong?

"Don't look so scared, it's going to all work out," Mom says, gently prodding me with her elbow.

"But what if…" I rub my hands together, trying to get rid of the clamminess.

"Drinks?" Peter steps up with two glasses of champagne and hands them to us.

"Thanks, that's very kind," Mom says, shooting him and me a smile. "I'm so glad you two managed to work things out. She was always a stubborn child, my Claudia."

"Mom!" I protest, my hands still shaking as I hold onto the champagne flute.

"So I've noticed," Peter jokes, placing his arm around my shoulder.

"It's about to start!" Mom remarks, after checking her watch. "I'm so proud of you, Claudia. I'm sure it will be a great success." She beams at me, her eyes sparkling with excitement.

I'm not so sure, so I just stand there, focused on breathing in and out, propping myself up against Peter's chest.

"Ladies and gentlemen, thank you so much for coming to our grand opening!" Lauren steps up in front of the crowd that has started collecting all around us. The beginning of her speech is met with polite applause. Towards my left, Mom takes my hand, squeezing it excitedly.

"For this landmark occasion, I'm very excited to announce a brand new addition to our line-up for tonight. Due to the last minute addition, she's not mentioned in the brochure. A fresh entrant into the local art scene, Claudia de Wit!"

Mom lets go of me, and applauds excitedly, causing a few bystanders to turn around and look at us. "Love you, sweetheart!" she whispers while I try to resist the urge to run.

"Of course we welcome familiar names as well tonight, including Tess Burgundy, and…" Lauren continues, pausing for the occasional applause when appropriate, introducing the rest of the artists included in the exhibit. I'm in amazing company, having seen some of the works earlier when they were still being set up.

As soon as the speech is over, everyone gets the chance to mingle and look around at the displays. I'm not sure at all what to do or where to go, so I just awkwardly stand around until Peter practically forces me to talk to some of the other exhibitors. Networking, he says. Awkwardness is more like it.

Just when I'm doing my best to strike up a conversation with a rather nice lady old enough to be my grandmother who paints still lifes, Lauren comes up towards me with a big grin on her face.

"Wonderful news, Claudia. You've made your first sale already!" She holds out her hand, which I shake in a daze.

"Which canvas?"

"*Summer Moon.*"

I'm speechless. That's the one they valued the highest at more than two grand! More than what I'd make in a month in my old job even after deducting tax.

"Congratulations. We'll get the paperwork drawn up as soon as possible as well as a check when the buyer finalizes everything."

"Who bought it?" I stammer, preparing myself for it to be Peter, in which case I'm going to go nuts.

"You see the man over there, in the pinstriped suit?" Lauren asks, gesturing subtly towards the far end of the gallery towards a small cluster of people. "His name is Callum Byrne."

I nod, still skeptical that some stranger is actually happy to shell out that kind of money for a creation of mine. The man turns around, and raises his champagne glass in our direction. He looks vaguely familiar, but I can't place him. Could it be one of Peter's colleagues whom I met at the race event? No, that doesn't seem right...

"He said it will be the perfect centerpiece for a new restaurant he's planning on opening next year." Lauren gives him a little wave, which the man acknowledges before turning back to chat to his elegant female companion. "A good, regular customer of ours. I'm so pleased he's taken a liking to your work." She smiles at me and turns around to mingle some more.

I'm still shocked. He owns a restaurant? Where have I seen his face before?

"What did I miss?" Peter asks, offering me a new glass of champagne.

"That guy over there bought the moon painting. To hang in his restaurant apparently." I can't work out where I know him from.

"Wonderful! I'll drink to that." He holds up his glass, clinking it to mine. "I'd hate to say *I told you so*..."

"Oh, you!" I give him a playful slap on his arm, but I have to admit that for a change it's nice not to be right.

By the time the event is over, another two canvases have sold, and I'm about to be a lot richer than I was only hours ago. We say our goodbyes to

Mom, then make our way back to Peter's flat, arm in arm.

"That went surprisingly well," I remark.

He winks at me while unlocking his front door.

"I never doubted that it would."

"That makes one of us. I love you, Peter." I tiptoe and give him a kiss right on the lips.

"Love you too." He returns my kiss. "So, any idea what you're going to spend your newfound riches on?"

I just grin in response, knowing very well what I plan to do with at least some of the money while keeping a sensible amount for the inevitable rainy day. I sure hope he still wants to travel, because I hear Egypt is lovely this time of year and I've always wanted to see the Great Pyramids…

If all this success is just temporary, I can always restart the job hunt when we get back.

***

AUTHOR'S NOTE

Thanks so much for reading *Beautiful Stranger!*

This story holds a special place in my heart, because my entire writing career started with what is now the beginning of this novella. Back in October 2012, I took a deep breath, closed my eyes, crossed my fingers and even my toes, and clicked 'Publish' on a short story called *Ladies' Day*. Although I've made a few changes and additions, and unpublished the original, the same story is still present in Chapters 1 to 5 of this book you're reading now. It was the first thing I ever finished and offered for sale, and as such, the biggest milestone I have to show for as an author.

A lot has changed in the past few years. I like to think I've grown as a writer, and with it, my stories have developed. What started as a fun little encounter between a down-to-earth twenty-something girl, Claudia, and a middle class man fifteen years her senior has grown into something a lot more serious. Their relationship developed into something I couldn't have foreseen at the time.

We all want different things out of life, and it's so difficult to reconcile these hopes and dreams with those of another person. When Peter and Claudia first meet, they're both adrift, especially Peter. Claudia isn't quite as focused as she would want herself to believe, just going with the flow and hoping her job keeps providing the steady pay she so desperately craves. Towards the end of the story, obviously this is no longer the case and they're both in need of different future plans.

They complement each other. Claudia's backpacking experiences give Peter an idea for what he wants to spend his life doing more of: exploring the world. And Peter's encouragements finally get through to Claudia until she's willing to try out something she hadn't considered viable before: attempt to make a living from her art. She learns that one doesn't always have to be completely sensible and safe. Taking risks is OK, as long as it's not recklessly done.

I can relate to her fear that she isn't good enough to sell her paintings, and that she'll struggle to make a living selling the odd canvas here and there. It's not easy taking something you've created and expose it to other people, risking rejection and judgement. That's how I felt when I published that first story: uncertain whether it was up to scratch, and incredibly grateful when people actually bought and enjoyed it. Hopefully you, the reader, could relate to her as well.

BEAUTIFUL STRANGER

Beautiful Stranger could have easily become a fairytale story, about an ordinary girl swept off her feet by a handsome older guy who showers her with gifts and ensures she never has to worry about money ever again. Of course, not everyone can accept that kind of thing, least of all Claudia who has always fended for herself. And would such an arrangement work long term? Would Peter never have wondered if perhaps she only liked him for his money? I think he might have, so they had to find another way...

Enough of all these rambling thoughts. I hope you enjoyed the story as much as I did while writing it, and if you're interested in reading more of my work, perhaps you'll consider signing up for my newsletter. I'll even give you a free book of your choice when you sign up!

x, Lorelei

- ❖ LMoone.com
- ❖ Lorelei Moone on Facebook
- ❖ AuthorLMoone on Instagram

I also write Paranormal Romance as Lorelei Moone. Check out LoreleiMoone.com for more information.

Printed in Great Britain
by Amazon